My ~~first~~ Forever Love

D. E. Haggerty

Copyright © 2022 D.E. Haggerty

All rights reserved.

D.E. Haggerty asserts the moral right to be identified as the author of this work.

ISBN: 9798436812656

My Forever Love is a work of fiction. The names, characters, places, and incidents portrayed in it are the product of the author's imagination. Any resemblance to actual persons, living or dead, events or locations is entirely coincidental.

All rights reserved. No part of this publication may be reproduced, stored in a retrieval system, or transmitted, in any form or by any means, electronic, mechanical, photocopying, recording or otherwise, without the prior permission of the author.

No portion of this book may be reproduced in any form without written permission from the publisher or author, except as permitted by U.S. copyright law.

Also by D.E. Haggerty

Forever For You
Just For Forever
Stay For Forever
Only Forever
Meet Disaster
Meet Not
Meet Dare
Meet Hate
Bragg's Truth
Bragg's Love
Perfect Bragg
Bragg's Match
Bragg's Christmas
How to Date a Rockstar
How to Love a Rockstar
How to Fall For a Rockstar
How to be a Rockstar's Girlfriend
How to Catch a Rockstar
A Hero for Hailey
A Protector for Phoebe

A Soldier for Suzie
A Fox for Faith
A Christmas for Chrissie
A Valentine for Valerie
A Love for Lexi
About Face
At Arm's Length
Hands Off
Knee Deep
Molly's Misadventures

Chapter 1

Bad day – the point at which even the most well-adjusted person snaps

Shit. Police lights in my rearview mirror is not the welcome home I was hoping for.

"Uh-oh, Waffles, the Fuzz is on our tail."

My dog lifts his head, peers outside for a second, decides outside is not worth his time, gives a mini-woof, and goes back to his nap.

"I guess I'm on my own," I mutter.

I check the speedometer, but I'm positive I wasn't speeding. This piece of trash car can barely make it up to the speed limit without shimmying and shaking like it's going to fall into pieces right in the middle of the road. I'd be a complete idiot to drive faster than absolutely necessary. And, despite current appearances, I am not a complete idiot.

Plus, I know once I pass the sign for Winter Falls – the world's first carbon neutral town – I need to slow down or risk a ticket. There are no warnings for speeding in a town of people who think using fossil fuels is equivalent to mass murder. Decarbonization is serious business in these parts.

I pull to the shoulder and watch the police officer as he exits his vehicle and swaggers toward me. Oh my. The ugly uniform is doing nothing to hide the delicious thighs he's sporting. My gaze roves higher to his narrow hips. Moving back to home – albeit temporarily – doesn't seem so bad right now.

He stops next to my window and my gaze lifts until it hits his name badge. *No. No. No. No. It can't be.* I force myself to continue raising my head until I can view his face. Damnit. It is. Lyric Alston. Town bad boy. Town hottie. And the boy who shattered my heart into a million pieces. Awesome. Freaking awesome.

"Roll down your window, Aspen!"

Oh, right. Lyric isn't merely the 'boy who shattered my heart', he's also the Chief of Police of Winter Falls, Colorado. Population – 1,001.

I start cranking the window down. No electric windows on this luxury vehicle of mine. Naturally, the stupid handle falls off in my hand, and I end up dropping it. Ugh! Can this day get any worse?

I bend over to search for the handle when my door unexpectedly opens, and I tumble out of the car into Lyric's arms. I had to ask if this day could get any worse, didn't I?

"Still haven't learned to wear a seatbelt, Aspen?"

I shove him away and scramble to my feet. "I was wearing a seatbelt, officer," I sneer. "I unhooked it when I came to a stop. I know better than to get trapped in a car during a traffic stop."

He frowns. "Of course. How could I forget Winter Falls isn't big enough for Aspen West? Only the city is good enough for you."

I don't respond. Why bother? We had this argument at least ten gazillion times after we graduated from college, and I wanted to move to New York City or Denver or anywhere but Winter Falls. Lyric had zero interest in moving. He was all set to settle down in our hometown, get married, and have a bunch of kids. The discussion of other possibilities was not on the table.

"Why'd you pull me over, Lyric?"

He taps the roof of the car. "This vehicle is not roadworthy."

Tell me about it. I didn't think I was going to manage the drive from Dallas to my hometown, but I didn't have any money for anything better. As it is, I had to sell some of my jewelry to buy this piece of crap.

"You know vehicles with gasoline engines are strictly limited in Winter Falls."

The joys of living in a carbon neutral town. Don't get me wrong. I'm all for green energy and saving the environment but being a savior of the planet is expensive. I would have had to sell *all* of my jewelry to afford an electric car and since I'm currently homeless, out of money, and out of a job, I had no intention of spending more money than was absolutely necessary.

"Can you give me a break this one time, Lyric?"

"It's Chief Alston."

"Really? You're pulling rank on me right now?" I bite my tongue before I call him a fathead power abusing son of a goat farmer.

"It's not pulling rank when it's true."

He leans over to peer into my backseat, and I block him. Everything I own is in this car. I left this town with hopes of taking the world by storm. I never expected to return ten years later while driving a thirty-year-old car with all of my possessions able to fit in its trunk and backseat. The last thing I need is for Lyric stupid head Alston to see me at my lowest.

I spot the orange stains on my yoga pants. Maybe that particular ship has already sailed.

"What's going on, Miss Big City? Did you crash and burn?"

I flinch at the word burn. It's a miracle I'm standing here alive and not burnt to a crisp. Lucky for me, Waffles needed to go out to pee at two o'clock in the morning. If he hadn't? I shiver. I don't want to think about what would have happened had I been in my apartment sleeping when the fire broke out.

As if he knows I'm thinking about him, my dog barks at me from the front passenger seat.

"Hold on, Waffles. We'll go for a walk soon."

"Waffles? You named your dog Waffles?"

Was Lyric always such a pain in the butt jerk? Was I too enamored with his brown, wavy locks of hair and sky-blue eyes that I ignored all the signs of him being a dickhead?

I cross my arms over my chest, and his eyes dip briefly to my breasts. Yep, I totally missed the signs of dickhead. Good thing I'm no longer sixteen and have built up immunity to broad-shouldered, narrow-waisted, strong-thighed men, who happen to be six-foot-three and eternally tan.

"For your information, Chief of Police who couldn't find a clue if it hit him in the face, Waffles is a rescue. I found him behind my building. The sole way I could get his shaking, scared out of his mind, furry butt to come near me was to offer him waffles. Thus, Waffles."

He grimaces. "Shit. You're right. I'm sorry. And Waffles is adorable."

You bet he is. He's my baby.

"You took me by surprise is all. I didn't expect you to be in town this time of year is all."

Relief rushes through me. My family has kept my secret. It's nothing short of a miracle. I half expected the entire town to be waiting to greet my return. No, not return. I'm not here for good. I'm not staying any longer than it takes for the insurance company to stop dragging its feet.

"Small town gossip has failed you, *Chief*." I emphasize Chief and a muscle in his jaw spasms before he whips out his citation book and flips it open.

"I'm sorry, Aspen, but I'm going to have to write you a ticket for driving an unapproved gasoline engine vehicle."

A ticket I won't be able to afford. I knew using all my savings to expand my business and buy the café next door to the bookstore was a gamble. I just didn't realize how big a gamble it would be until everything burned down.

"Can't you give me a warning this one time, Chief?"

He shakes his head. "Policy says otherwise. No warnings for residents of Winter Falls."

"I'm not technically a resident," I'm quick to point out.

He rips the ticket off of the pad and holds it out to me. "You grew up here. You can't claim to be ignorant of the rules."

I bite my lip as I stare down at the ticket as if it's a snake set on biting me and infecting me with its poison. I retreat a step. There's got to be some way for me to get out of this. I'm not commemorating my return – however temporary it may be – home with a ticket.

I look around hoping the field surrounding town can offer me a solution to this problem. My gaze stops when I notice the *Welcome to Winter Falls* sign. I'm parked about twenty feet in front of it, meaning I'm not within the town limits.

I don't bother trying to hide my grin. "I'm sorry, Chief, but I think I'm going to have to decline your ticket."

He waves the ticket he's still holding at me. "You can't decline a ticket, Aspen. It doesn't matter how much we meant to each other as kids."

Meant? As in past tense? Ouch. My heart clenches, but I ignore it.

"I'm not trying to abuse our past relationship." I point to the sign, and he swears under his breath.

"If I hadn't stopped you, you would have driven straight past the sign."

My grin widens. "But, thanks to you, I didn't."

"What are you going to do? You can't leave your vehicle on the side of the road."

Because he would take way too much pleasure in writing me a ticket for abandoning my vehicle. Not going to happen.

"I'll call Basil to tow it." Basil owns the only tow truck in town.

He rips the ticket in half. "You better call Basil. I won't hesitate to write you another ticket."

Of course, he won't. I want to ask him who shoved the stick up his bum, but I think I've antagonized him enough for today especially since he currently looks ready to throw me into a jail cell.

"Have a good day, Chief. Thanks for stopping by to remind me of the town ordinances."

I try to tone down my sarcasm, but judging by the thunder in Lyric's face, I'm not entirely successful. Despite how he broke my heart when I left town after our college graduation, we've been civil to each other whenever I've been back home visiting my family. I have a sneaking suspicion our days of being civil have come to an end.

He tilts his hat. "Good day, Aspen."

Despite what a rule following son of a gun he is, I can't stop myself from watching him walk away. The way the muscles in his ass bunch as he moves should be illegal.

But it doesn't matter how gorgeous Lyric Alston is, the man is not to be trusted. He's a heartbreaker, and the last thing my heart needs right now is another break.

Chapter 2

Family tree – a diagram showing your relationship to all the nuts in your family.

WHEN WE PULL UP into my parent's driveway in Basil's beast – as he affectionately refers to his tow truck – my entire family is waiting for me on the front porch. There goes my hope for keeping my return home quiet.

"Thanks for the ride, Basil."

"No problem, man. No problem."

With his long hair, bell-bottom pants, and bright floral shirt, Basil resembles a hippie headbanger, which is fitting since he totally is. The first generation of Winter Springs residents are all hippies. It made for an interesting childhood.

My door flies open. "Aspen Cloud, you're home."

My mom sounds happy, so I don't bother reminding her of how much I hate the name Cloud or how I'm not home for good. I'm home for now anyway. I climb out of Basil's beast straight into her arms.

Mom's arms wrap around me, and she sways me from side to side. "I can't tell you how happy I am to see you."

I close my eyes and sink into the comfort she's offering. The fear and tension I've been feeling since I saw the flames shooting out of my building ease out of me. I'm home. I'm safe. I have somewhere to sleep tonight besides the backseat of my car.

She leans back to gaze into my eyes. "You're going to be fine, baby girl. Just fine."

For the first time since my home and business were destroyed, I believe it. "Thanks, Mom."

Dad elbows Mom out of the way and lifts me into his arms before twirling me around like I'm the seven-year-old girl who thinks playing helicopter is the best thing in the world, instead of the thirty-three-year-old mature adult I am. I giggle as he spins me around. Maybe not a mature adult then.

"Put me down, Dad. I'm not a child." There's no heat in my words since I'm giggling like the seven-year-old girl I claim I'm not.

He sets me on the ground and places his forehead against mine. "You'll always be a child to me, baby girl."

"Thanks, Daddy-O."

"Stop hogging her!"

My sisters, all four of them, attack and I don't stand a chance. Before I know it, we're rolling around on the ground.

"It's good to have you home, big sis," Ellery says.

The others – Juniper, Lilac, and Ashlyn – murmur their agreement. In case it's unclear, my parents were hippies – still are actually – and they named their five girls after their five favorite trees. You'd think we'd get teased about it, but in the town of Winter Springs, hippie names are the norm.

I'm the oldest of this gang of sisters with Ellery next. Lilac is smack dab in the middle. Then, comes Juniper and last but not least is Ashlyn.

Woof!

I struggle to my feet. "I need to let Waffles out before he pees all over the interior of my car."

Lilac, aka Ms. Civil Engineer, curls her lip at the state of my car. "This is your vehicle? It's in violation of town ordinance."

I roll my eyes. "Yes, Ms. Know It All, but I didn't exactly have a ton of cash laying around to buy a car when my life burned to the ground. Literally."

She flinches. "Sorry, Aspen. I didn't mean …" She clears her throat. "Anyway, I assume Basil will be removing this eyesore from the driveway."

"Geez, Lilac. Have some compassion." Ashlyn bumps her shoulder as she passes her to open the passenger door of my car.

Waffles jumps out of the car, dashes to the lawn, does three circles, and promptly lifts his leg to have a wee. While pee is still streaming out of him, he notices a squirrel on the lawn and rushes after it leaving a trail of pee in his wake.

The squirrel scurries up a tree, and Waffles paws at the tree while barking up a storm at the poor squirrel. At least, he's finally done peeing.

"I got him," Juniper – my animal loving sister – yells. "You unload the car."

She holds out a treat to Waffles and he swivels away from the tree toward Juniper. She keeps the treat out in front of her as she backs into the house with my dog eagerly following her.

"Is this everything?" Dad asks from where he's peering into the trunk.

"Yeah," I sigh out.

Ellery wraps her arm around me. "It could have been worse."

Staring at the three boxes of books and one suitcase of clothes comprising every single thing I own in the world, I have a hard time believing her.

She squeezes my shoulder. "You're alive. You're young and you can rebuild."

"Easy for you to say. You have a successful business. I have nothing."

Ellery owns the local bed and breakfast. She spent years renovating the delipidated mansion on the southern edge of downtown and turned it into a romantic country inn – *The Inn on Main*.

"Yeah, well, owning a B&B is not all it's cracked up to be," she mutters under her breath.

Before I have a chance to ask her what she's talking about, she grabs my suitcase and marches into the house.

"What's going on with her?" I ask Ashlyn.

There's no sense asking Lilac. Ms. Engineer barely deigns to acknowledge the world outside of environmental engineering exists, she's hardly going to know why Ellery's unhappy.

Ashlyn frowns as she watches Ellery retreat into the house. "Rumor has it she's had some trouble with guests who don't approve of the no gasoline engine cars in town rule."

"It's utterly ridiculous," Lilac says. "There are free bikes anyone can use. And if a bike isn't good enough for her guests, they can rent an electric golf cart."

As part of the whole carbon neutral town thing, alternate forms of transportation are not simply encouraged, they're facilitated. Biking paths and footpaths are as prevalent – if not more prevalent – than roads for cars.

My parents – as do most residents – use a golf cart as their main source of transportation. They don't actually own a car – no one in my family does – which is why I had to buy this heaping pile of shit, to begin with.

Once we've emptied the car and placed my boxes and suitcase in my childhood bedroom, we gather at the dining room table where Mom has an apple pie waiting for us. Mom thinks apple pie heals all wounds. Her pie kind of does.

"What happened?" Ashlynn asks. "Why did your bookstore and apartment burn down?"

In addition to being a troublemaker of the highest order – something she's very proud of – my youngest sister was born without the tact gene.

Ellery squeezes my hand. "You don't have to answer her."

"It's fine."

I'm lying. It's not. I can still smell smoke in the air despite having showered and scrubbed my skin until it was raw several times since the fire. I practically used an entire bottle of shampoo on my hair trying to get the smell of smoke out of it. All to no avail.

I swallow and force myself to tell the story, albeit a much shorter version. "Waffles woke me up in the middle of the night because he needed to go out. When we returned, there were flames shooting out of the café and bookstore downstairs. I rushed upstairs and managed to throw some clothes and jewelry in a suitcase and put some of my photo albums and books in a few boxes."

"You went into a burning building?" Dad roars.

"Only the ground floor was actually burning. There weren't any flames in my apartment above."

"You could have been killed."

At his words, I draw the sleeves of my t-shirt down over my hands. Wrong move. My mother would have made the perfect Cold War spy. Ironic since she married a Soviet immigrant. She doesn't miss a thing. She shackles my wrist and carefully draws the material up my arm.

Her bottom lip trembles and there are tears in her eyes. "You didn't tell us you were injured."

"It's fine. They're barely second-degree burns."

"Second-degree burns can cause scarring," Lilac offers. When everyone at the table turns to stare at her, her eyes round. "What? It's a fact. You can't get mad at me for stating facts."

I sigh. "I'm not mad at you, Lilac Bean."

Mom stands. "Let me phone Dr. Blue. I'm certain we can get you an appointment right away."

"There's no need. I've already seen a doctor. He gave me antibiotics. Everything's fine."

Mom looks to Lilac for confirmation. At her nod, Mom returns to the table. "But you need to promise to tell me if you're in pain."

"I promise."

I'm sorry, Ashlyn mouths at me. I smile at her. It's not her fault. If she was in a fire, I'd want to know everything, too.

"Now," my dad says once the pie is demolished, "tell me why your insurance company won't pay out your claim."

Dad may appear to be a laidback hippie most of the time, but he's also the town's attorney. And he doesn't let anyone mess with his girls.

I shrug. "Since the cause of the fire is unclear, they need to conduct an arson investigation and eliminate me as a suspect before they'll pay my claim."

"Are they out of their minds?" Dad bellows.

Mom pats his arm. "Now, now, Daniel. Getting your heart rate up will not help anything."

When Mom isn't spying on or interrogating us until we spill all our secrets, she's the peacemaker. She's the principal of the local school and has plenty of experience keeping the peace. Lucky for me, she wasn't the principal when I was in school. It's hard to get away with skipping class when Mom's the principal.

"Besides," she smirks at me, "our baby girl is home until the insurance company pays the claim."

You don't need to be a mind reader to figure out what she's thinking. Mom hasn't exactly been subtle about her desire I return home for good. She never wanted me to leave in the first place.

She's out of luck. As soon as the insurance money is in my bank account, I'm out of here.

Chapter 3

Embarrass – what parents do to their children without even trying

LYRIC

I stand in front of the West family home with the orchid in my hands and wonder if this is the most epically stupid thing I've done in my life. Other than making fun of the mess in Aspen's car when those things were literally the only belongings she has in the world. Yeah, I'm an asshole.

Before I can make up my mind one way or the other, the door opens.

"You want me to get you a cup of coffee while you make up your mind?" Mrs. West asks.

I'm the Chief of Police of this town and yet the mother of my childhood sweetheart can make me feel about six inches tall. It's a gift she doesn't hesitate to use.

"I was—"

"Wondering whether approaching my oldest daughter was a mistake," she fills in.

I can't begin to explain how happy I am she wasn't the principal when I went to school. With her apparent ability to read my mind, I never would have graduated, let alone gone on to college.

I clear my throat. "I couldn't remember if Aspen is fond of orchids."

I'm a bald-faced liar. I know Aspens loves orchids.

Mrs. West doesn't call me on my obvious lie. "Come on in and we'll find out."

She ushers me through the house to the kitchen. "Sit. I'll get you a coffee."

The kitchen hasn't changed one bit since I was a teenager and used to join the West family for Sunday afternoon meals. The plain wood cabinets don't quite shut properly, and the floor is uneven. The result of Mr. West deciding to build the family home himself. Thank goodness he kept his attempts to the kitchen. Otherwise, I'm not sure the house would still be standing. Aspen's dad is a brilliant legal mind, but carpentry is beyond his skillset.

Mrs. West places a cup of coffee in front of me. "Aspen will be right out," she says with a wink before disappearing.

A few moments later Aspen stumbles into the kitchen with her eyes practically closed. She's wearing a pair of sweatpants with a hole in the knee and a long-sleeved t-shirt with the collar ripped out of it. Coupled with the mess of curls in her hair, it's obvious she just woke up.

And she couldn't be more beautiful. Her deep green eyes that spit fire when she's mad together with her black, curly hair are just the beginning. She also has a slightly upturned nose and a beauty mark above her left lip. A beauty mark I've licked more times than I can count.

Speaking of licking, Aspen has a body any red-blooded straight man would want to get his mouth on. She's no skinny girl who lives on salads. No, my Aspen—

I shut down those thoughts. Aspen isn't mine anymore. She hasn't been in a long time. Ever since she chose running away from Winter Falls over me. My stomach sours. Time to get this visit over with.

I clear my throat. "Good morning, Aspen."

She shrieks and the coffee cup in her hand falls to the floor. It shatters into pieces, and coffee splashes her legs.

"Freaking ow. As if I don't already have enough burned skin."

I freeze at her words. No one said anything about burns. I know her business and apartment burned down, but nobody said she was injured. I scan her body and notice her forearms are covered in bandages, not a long-sleeved t-shirt as I first thought.

I stand and approach her, being careful I don't step on any shards of glass, before bending to pick her up.

"Hey! What are you doing?" She slaps at my shoulders, but I ignore her.

"I'm making sure you don't step on anything sharp and cut yourself."

She deflates. "Oh. Okay. Thank you."

I can tell the words cost her, but I don't say anything. She's close to the family jewels, and I know for a fact the woman knows how to use her knee to create the most damage. My idiot brother still complains about 'phantom pains' from the time she kneed him for making fun of her braces.

I set her down on a chair and kneel in front of her. I reach for her leg, but she scoots away from me.

"What are you doing?" She hisses at me. "It's not get Aspen naked time. Those days are gone. Long gone."

She doesn't have to remind me. Whenever she's around, I'm reminded of those stolen moments we spent in each other's arms until it all went to shit.

"Are you burnt?" I ask instead.

"It's fine. A bit of coffee isn't going to hurt me."

I stare into her eyes. "You're positive you aren't hurt? I can have you in Dr. Blue's office in minutes."

"Yes, Chief," she snarls. "I'm positive."

I wince at the venom in her words. I never should have pulled rank on her during yesterday's traffic stop. In my defense, I hadn't been expecting to find her in the car. She's never visited Winter Falls in August before. She keeps to a strict schedule of visits – Christmas, Easter, July 4th.

I promise I'm not a stalker. I keep her schedule so I can shore up my defenses for when she's near. Otherwise, I may forget all about how she abandoned me without a single word and drop to my knees and beg her to return to town. Great. Now I sound like a lovesick sap.

I stand. "Stay there. I'll pick up the mess and get you a new cup of coffee."

I sop up the mess with a towel before sweeping up the coffee cup shards. I don't throw them away, though. In Winter Falls, throwing away pottery shards is equal to blasphemy. I find a paper bag under the sink and place the ruined coffee cup in it. I'll give the bag to our local mosaic artist later.

"What are you doing here anyway?" Aspen asks when I set a new coffee cup in front of her.

I sit across from her before answering. "I came to apologize."

Her eyes narrow. "You came to apologize? Does the Chief of Police make house calls now?"

"I'm sorry. I shouldn't have pulled rank on you."

She waves away my apology. "You were right. You are the chief." She takes a breath and lets it out before continuing, "I'm happy for you by the way. Being Chief of Police is everything you always wanted."

Not everything. I also want a wife and a bunch of rugrats running around my house. It hasn't happened yet, though, and at the age of thirty-three, I'm starting to worry it never will. Unless— Nope. I put the breaks on those thoughts. Aspen is not to be trusted. She'll only abandon me again.

"I came to apologize about something else."

She cocks her eye. "You did?"

"I was a dick about the car, especially considering what's happened."

She groans before allowing her head to fall to the table. "I hate small town life."

"Hey." I push her hair out of her eyes. "People aren't gossiping about what happened to you because they're mean. Everyone's worried about you."

She sits up. "Which is worse. I don't need everyone pitying me."

I nod to her forearms. "I think we have a right to be concerned."

She grunts. "They're barely second-degree burns. The chance of scarring is minimal."

I reach across the table to grasp her hand. I ignore the spark flowing from her soft skin to mine. "Second-degree burns hurt like a bitch. I should know."

She rolls her eyes. "Yeah, well, you deserved it. Why you ever thought you could walk on coals is beyond me."

I release her hand and lean back in my chair. "It didn't stop you from helping to set up the coals, though."

"And miss you acting like a total fool? No way."

"Hey! I made it at least halfway through before I gave up."

She snorts. "Halfway? You can't measure to save your life. Most men can't. It's why women don't know what six inches is anymore."

I ignore the burn of jealousy in my stomach at her mention of other men. I can hardly be jealous. I haven't been a saint in her absence. Quite the opposite, in fact. I may want to settle down, but until I find the right person – and the right person is *not* sitting in front of me no matter how many sparks fly between us when we touch – I'm going to enjoy myself.

I wiggle my eyebrows. "Six inches? As I recall, you never complained before."

The screen door bangs closed, and I glance over to find Aspen's youngest sister frozen with her nose pressed up against the screen.

"Mom! They're talking about sex. Make them stop."

Mrs. West strolls into the room. "Now, now, Ashlyn, don't be a prude. Sex is natural. It's one of the most beautiful ways to show a person you care for them." She wiggles her brows. "And it's awful fun, too."

Ashlyn slams her hands over her ears. "Na na na na. I can't hear you. My parents don't have sex."

Her mother smirks before tugging Ashlyn's hands away from her ears. "If I don't have sex with your father, how did we manage to create five wonderful daughters?"

"IVF? Immaculate conception? I don't know. But you do not have sex. Ever."

"What about the time you found them out by the waterfall, Ashlyn? What were they doing then?" Aspen asks her.

Ashlyn feigns gagging. "I have spent years with a therapist wiping those memories from my mind. You've ruined years of therapy!"

"Oh, please." Mrs. West rolls her eyes. "If you were having therapy sessions with Moonbeam, she would have told us."

Ashlyn throws her arms in the air. "She's not supposed to tell my parents I'm in therapy."

Mrs. West snorts. "Did you forget you live in Winter Falls?"

"How could I ever forget," Ashlyn mutters before tromping off down the hallway.

"I'm sorry," Mrs. West says. "I wanted to give you privacy, but I couldn't get to Ashlyn in time. I did try."

I stand. "It's fine, ma'am. I need to get back to work anyway."

My radio squawks in confirmation. I nod to Aspen. "It was nice seeing you."

My words may sound like a goodbye, but this is not a farewell no matter how much I may wish it were. Winter Falls is a small town. I'll come across her beautiful face all over town until she decides to leave and abandon me once again.

Chapter 4

Skinny dipping – a very bad idea if you don't guard your clothes

A HAND IS PLACED over my mouth, and my eyes fly open.

"We need to be quiet, big sis," Ellery orders in a whisper. I nod and she removes her hand.

"What are you doing here at …" I squint at the view out of my bedroom window to discover it's still pitch-black outside "… the middle of the night."

"Ms. Fancy Business Owner over here doesn't have any other time free during the day," Ashlyn mutters.

Ellery is quick with a snide comment back. "At least I have a business."

Pain flashes in Ashlyn's eyes before she turns away. I need to add 'talk to my baby sister about what's going on in her life' to the top of my to-do list. Since the rest of my to-do list is currently empty, I think I'll be able to slot her in somewhere.

"Here." Lilac shoves a sweatshirt in my hands. "You need to keep your burns covered until they're healed."

I sit up in bed. "Where are we going?" I don't wait for an answer before putting the sweatshirt on over my pajama top.

"To the falls, of course. It's tradition." Juniper rubs her hands together in anticipation.

"I don't remember going to the falls in the middle of the night on Lammas before."

Lammas, also known as Loaf Mass Day, is a day to celebrate the importance of the harvest. Normally, we bake bread and give thanks for the grains and first fruits of the harvest. There's also a street festival to mark the event.

"You haven't been around for August Eve in a decade, sis."

I shrug at Juniper's response. She's not wrong. I can hardly call in sick at work when I own the business. But the bookstore I spent years building is now in ashes. I shove those depressing thoughts aside in favor of paying attention to my sisters.

We sneak out of my bedroom and down the hallway toward the front door. I don't know why we're sneaking. We're all adults and my parents were never strict parents in the first place. Except for at school. At school, Teacher West thought she needed to set a good example.

I slide my bare feet into a pair of hiking boots before we slip out the backdoor. I make my way toward my parent's golf cart, but Ellery grabs my hand to stop me. "We're hiking."

Winter Falls isn't very far out of town. The waterfall is the whole reason for the town being settled at its current location. When the first generation of hippies saw the waterfall, they knew this was the place to grow their community.

They wanted to build a community completely off the grid and the waterfall was the perfect opportunity for power. It still is. Despite harnessing less than half of the potential hydroelectric power of the waterfall – because harnessing all of the power would have ecological implications the founders were not okay with – it's enough power to provide electricity for the entire town.

The solar panels on every house in town don't hurt either. Plus, there's the wind farm they added south of town a few years ago as the town's power needs grew. There's also a plan to use biomass to create energy, but don't ask me any questions about it since science is not my favorite subject. Lilac's the one to ask.

Juniper and Ashlyn don backpacks while Ellery and Lilac switch on flashlights to light our path.

As soon as we're away from the houses, I ask, "When did this become a tradition?"

Juniper points to Ashlyn. "When this one turned twenty-one two years ago."

"Because she wasn't sneaking out of the house and stealing drinks before then?"

Ashlyn hip checks me. "Alcohol is totally natural. In Europe, the legal drinking age is much younger than here, yet the level of alcoholism in the US is way higher."

"Way higher?" Lilac frowns at her. "This isn't a scientific term."

Ashlyn rolls her eyes. "We're not all scientific nerds."

"Is this supposed to offend me?" Lilac appears genuinely confused.

"A natural process the same way sex is a natural process? Especially sex between our parents," I tease my little sister.

She pretends to gag. "Stop. You're as bad as Mom."

"No one can be as bad as Mom. How old were you when she gave you the sex talk for the first time?"

"I was six. I'd never seen a penis, let alone understood boys have one, but there's Mom showing me a very graphic picture book explaining everything."

"Did you talk about this terrifying experience with your therapist?"

She sticks her tongue out at me. "I'm not in therapy."

"Good." I throw my arm around her. "Because Moonbeam would totally tell Mom about it."

"I don't understand how Moonbeam has any clients," Lilac comments. "Therapists are supposed to keep their sessions confidential."

Ellery holds up a hand. "Shush. I hear something."

Ellery and Lilac switch off their flashlights, and we join hands, so we don't lose each other in the dark. Dawn is approaching, but under the canopy of the forest, it's easy to get confused and lose your way.

I hear a splash. Is someone swimming in the river below the falls? There's a reason the falls are nicknamed Winter Falls. Because they are 'freeze your toes off' cold. It might be the middle of summer, but I'm certain those waters haven't warmed up much.

Ashlyn tugs on my hand. "Come on. I wonder who it is."

We hike in a line behind her until we come to a clearing near the water. We duck down behind the brush before anyone can spot us.

Ashlyn peeks around the brush and sighs. "Oh my."

"What is it?"

"You need to see for yourself."

I rise up on my tiptoes to peek over the brush. Lyric and his brothers River and Phoenix are swimming in the water. As I watch, Lyric climbs out of the water and my eyes nearly bug out of their sockets. He's naked. The muscles in his thighs and ass bunch as he climbs the rocks on the opposite side of the river. Oh my. When he starts to turn around, I duck back down.

"They're all naked," I whisper-shout to my sisters.

"Who?" Ellery asks but doesn't wait for my response before standing up to have a look for herself.

I yank her down before she can see Lyric in all his glory. And I do mean glory. I have first-hand proof of the glory as it were.

"It's Aspen's boyfriend," she sings.

"Boyfriend?" Lilac's nose wrinkles in confusion. "No one told me you have a new boyfriend."

Ellery rolls her eyes. "I mean Lyric."

"Ah yes." Lilac nods. "The boy who got away."

I smack her. "He didn't get away. I'm the one who left."

"But now you're back, and you can pick up where you left off," Juniper says.

"Um, no. There will be no picking up where we left off. Lyric and I are done."

"Which is why you're blushing, and your heart rate has increased upon witnessing him naked."

I glare at Lilac. How dare she use science to prove I'm not over Lyric? "Whatever."

"You should have a summer fling with him," Ashlyn suggests.

"What is this? Pick on Aspen day. I'm the big sister here. I should be doing the picking, not you guys."

"Oh, oh a summer romance," Juniper sings.

"I think the song is *Bad Romance* and trust me the idea of Lyric and I together is a bad romance."

"You don't need to have a romance. You can use him for sex," Ellery suggests, and I smack her. "What? You haven't turned into a prude living in Dallas, have you?"

"Sex with my high school boyfriend. What a great idea." Not. It's a one-way trip to heartbreak hotel.

She rubs her hands together. "Awesome. Let's make this happen." She starts to stand, and I yank her down again.

"I was joking." She damn well knows I was joking, but she does love to push my buttons. What is it about siblings? They know exactly which buttons to push, and they have no problems pushing them.

"I think it's a good idea," Lilac says, and everyone turns to stare at her. "What? I've had sex."

Ashlyn groans. "Doesn't anyone keep their sex lives private anymore?"

"Anymore?" Juniper snorts. "Where have you been? No one in Winter Falls has ever kept their sex lives private."

"Yeah." Ellery nods in agreement. "If anything, they brag about their sex lives."

"And if Aspen has sex with Lyric maybe she can finally get over him," Lilac adds.

"Get over him? I'm over him," I claim.

She purses her lips. "Your irritation every time his name is mentioned leads me to a different conclusion."

"Whatever." I search my mind for a way out of this awkward conversation. I grin when I come up with the perfect solution. "Are we going to sit here gabbing all morning or are we going to steal the Alstons' clothes?"

Ellery smirks. "I'm in."

I point to her. "You create a diversion while I grab the clothes." At her nod, I continue. "The rest of you run in three different directions, so they don't know who to follow."

"This is a silly plan." I glare at Lilac until she sighs. "Fine. I'm in."

I crawl on my hands and knees until I reach the boulder where the brothers left their discarded clothes. I check to make sure the men don't notice me, but they're too busy fighting about who can jump from the highest point.

As I watch, Lyric uses his arms to propel himself out of the water. Those arm muscles are nearly as delicious as his thighs. When he spins around and his manhood is exposed, I sigh. *Oh my.* My memories have not exaggerated his size.

"Don't do it, Aspen!" he yells across the water. *Shit.* Did I sigh out loud? "She's stealing our clothes," he tattles to his brothers and points to me.

His brothers waste no time starting to swim across the river toward me.

I quickly gather the clothes into my arms and jump to my feet. "Run!"

Where's Ellery and her diversion? She's standing frozen staring at the men swimming toward us. Not helpful.

"Ellery, diversion!"

She jolts before waving her arms around. "Help! I need help!"

If there's one thing the Alston boys can't resist, it's a woman in distress. Their focus shifts from me to her, and I bolt. I run as fast as I can considering I'm wearing hiking boots and my boobs are bouncing all over the place since I'm not wearing a bra.

Lilac is waiting for me at the end of the trail with a golf cart. "Hop on." She pats the seat next to her.

"This is why I stick to science," she grumbles as she drives us to our parent's house. "Experiments don't chase you when you fail."

I burst out laughing. "Maybe not, but this is way more fun."

"You may have a point."

Chapter 5

Festival – a celebration to commemorate a special occasion; often used as an excuse to drink and be merry

ELLERY RETURNS TO THE inn, but Lilac, Juniper, Ashlyn, and I make our way downtown for the annual Lammas festival. Main Street is lined with local businesses – no chain stores here – and each business has set up a booth on the sidewalk in front of their storefront to display their wares.

"No parade this year?" I ask as we turn onto Main Street.

"There was some problem between the chamber of commerce and the police department. You should ask your boyfriend about it." Ashlyn wiggles her eyebrows at me.

"How many times do I have to tell you he isn't my boyfriend?"

"I would say until your heartrate stops increasing each time Lyric Alston is mentioned," Lilac surmises.

Before I can respond, I hear my name called from across the street. "Aspen Cloud West as I live and breathe."

Oh boy. Here we go. I put a smile on my face and wave. "Hi, Petal! How are you?"

"I'll be better when you get over here and give me a hug."

"How's business going?" I ask once we've hugged.

Petal flourishes her hand toward the homemade candles she makes. "Can I interest you in a candle? I have massage candles and wax play candles."

Yes, you heard her correctly. Petal doesn't sell any 'normal' candles at her store, *Sensual Scents*. She deals exclusively in sex candles.

"No thanks."

She's not to be deterred. "This massage candle is filled with the essential oils of rose and lavender, which have aphrodisiac properties."

She doesn't let me respond before she's holding up a different candle. "And this wax play candle is soy-based to avoid stinging. But, if you want some extra sting, I have paraffin candles as well."

I hold up my hands. "Petal, I don't have anyone to use those candles with."

She winks. "What about our fine Chief of Police?"

"Yeah, Aspen. Why don't you buy some candles just in case?" Ashlyn taunts.

I open my mouth to respond but slam it shut again when I realize no matter what I say, she's going to tease me about Lyric. I need to stop letting her push my buttons, and I have the perfect idea.

I shove the sleeves up on my long-sleeved t-shirt. "I don't think wax play is for me after what happened." I add a sniff at the end of the sentence to really sell it.

Petal gasps. "Oh my, dear. I'm sorry." She grabs a candle and hands it to me. "Here, this is an aromatherapy candle. It should soothe you. No cost."

"I can't—"

"I won't hear another word. Now, go have some fun." She leaves to help a couple who are perusing her wax play candle display before I can respond.

"I can't believe you played the sympathy card." Juniper frowns at me.

Ashlyn bats her eyes at me while placing her hand on her heart. "I'm so proud of you, big sis."

Lilac glances between the three of us. "I'm confused."

Ashlyn rolls her eyes. "What's new?"

"Chipmunks!" Juniper exclaims before rushing off to the pet store's booth.

Unleashed is not a normal pet store. Oh sure, they have a grooming service and carry pet food, although all of the pet food is organic and homemade. Where they differ from other ordinary, everyday pet stores is in the animals they carry. They don't have dogs or cats. No, the animals they carry are all animals the owner, Forest, has rescued. You never know what creatures you'll find at his shop.

We follow Juniper to where she's oohing and aahing over a cage. Forest hates putting the animals in cages, but after the Great Gopher Outbreak of 2010, he agreed to use them.

"Ah, what a cute bunny." Ashlyn points to another enclosure.

"It's not a bunny, it's a snowshoe hare," Juniper corrects her.

She would know. The woman is crazy about animals of all kinds. She has been ever since I can remember. She used to bring all sorts of wild animals back to the house. Mom and Dad were fine with it until the 'cat' she brought home turned out to be a mountain lion. Then, they put their foot down.

As a self-proclaimed animal lover, working at the wildlife refuge outside of town is the perfect fit for Juniper. The refuge primarily houses wild animals people thought would make good pets. Once they realize wild animals are wild for a reason, they often end up at the refuge where my little sis babies them.

"How much for the chipmunk?" Juniper doesn't wait for a response from Forest before picking up the animal and cuddling it to her chest.

He frowns at her. "You know my animals are always free."

It's true. Forest doesn't put a price on pets, because – according to him – you can't attach a price tag to love.

"No." Ashlyn glares at Juniper. "You promised no more pets."

Ashlyn and Juniper live together. Personally, I can't imagine living with my sister, but they make it work – probably because Juniper practically lives at the wildlife refuge and Ashlyn does about a gazillion different odd jobs until she figures out what she wants to do with her life.

Juniper holds the little rodent up and bats her eyelashes at Ashlyn. "But he's so dang cute."

Ashlyn snorts. "You said those exact same words about a rattlesnake last week." She shivers. "A snake."

Juniper juts out her lower lip, but Ashlyn isn't giving on this. It makes me wonder how many animals they already have in their apartment. Scratch that. I don't what to know.

Juniper sighs and puts the chipmunk back in its enclosure. "Bye, Alvin. Until we meet again."

"Who wants ice cream?" I ask when I spot Feather's ice cream cart in front of her store *Feather's Frozen Delights*.

"It's ten a.m. No one eats ice cream at this time of day," Lilac the straitlaced points out.

"You do if it's Feather's ice cream."

Feather's ice cream is the best. She makes it herself with whatever fruits and berries are in season. You never know what wonderful flavors you'll encounter.

Ashlyn hooks her arm through my elbow. "I'm with Aspen."

She starts skipping and I have no choice but to skip with her since we're attached.

"Aspen Cloud!" Feather rounds her cart to give me a hug. This town is big on hugs.

"Welcome home. I heard you and Lyric are back together."

I rear back. "What?"

She rolls her eyes. "Going skinny dipping together in the moonlight spells relationship."

"Lyric and I weren't skinny dipping."

"Sure, you weren't." She winks at me. "What flavor can I get you? On the house." She frowns. "I am sorry about the troubles you've been having."

"Um, thanks. But Lyric and I really aren't back together." I feel the need to set things straight before the town rumor mill has me pregnant and married off.

Ashlyn elbows me out of the way. "Do I get a free ice cream cone, too? Or is the free ice cream offer exclusive for Aspen?"

"What flavors do you have?" Juniper asks.

"Can we get the facts straight about what happened this morning first?" I ask.

Ashlyn waves away my concern. "Maybe you weren't skinny dipping with Lyric this morning, but it'll happen. It's only a matter of time. Now, back to the flavors."

I open my mouth to speak, but Lilac stops me. "You might as well forget it. Even I know it's a lost cause."

"Whatever," I mumble under my breath.

"I have blackberry, blueberry, and plum today. What'll it be?" Feather asks.

Once everyone – including Ms. It's Too Early for Ice Cream – has a cone, we continue on.

"Geez, sis, you should let your business burn to the ground more often if everyone's going to give us free stuff," Ashlyn says.

"What an awesome plan. I'll let my building worth half a million dollars burn so you can get a five-dollar ice cream for free."

"Why is this a good plan? Did you subtract wrong?" Lilac asks.

"It's this thing known as sarcasm, sis."

She sighs. "I don't understand sarcasm."

"We know. We know," Juniper murmurs.

By now, we've reached the town square, which sits smackdab in the middle of Main Street. The square has a small park complete with a large tree and gazebo. My brow wrinkles when I notice what else is in the park today.

"Wow. Is someone going for the Guinness book of world records for the largest loaf of bread?"

"Don't be ridiculous. The largest loaf of bread weighed over three-thousand pounds." Naturally, Lilac knows how big the largest loaf of bread was. "In a town of one-thousand inhabitants, most of the bread would go to waste."

Waste is not okay in Winter Falls. Waste fills up landfills and ruins the environment. There are a million more reasons the town's founders don't believe in waste, but I've learned to tune out their lectures.

"It is the Lammas festival," Ashlyn remarks. "You can hardly have Loaf Mass Day without a big loaf of bread."

"Come on." Juniper motions us forward. "Let's get our share."

I start to follow them until I notice the Chief of Police is front and center helping with the distribution. No thanks. Before I have a chance to escape, though, Lilac is dragging me forward.

"You can't avoid him forever considering how small the town of Winter Falls is." Trust me, I know. I've tried. "You really should consider my suggestion of copulating with him to get him out of your system."

"Copulating? Way to make it sound romantic."

"Are you being sarcastic again?"

I trudge behind her and join the line of residents. Unfortunately, the line isn't long, and I don't have a chance to shore up my defenses before it's my turn.

"Aspen West, I should arrest you for stealing."

I bat my eyelashes. "Whatever do you mean, Chief? I'm positive our law-abiding police officer wasn't out skinny dipping and violating laws of public nudity."

He smirks. "There are no laws regarding public nudity in Winter Falls."

Shoot! How could I forget my hometown and its crazy public ordinances, or lack thereof in this case?

"You should arrest Aspen and throw her in jail, Lyric," someone in the crowd suggests. "Give her a good frisking, too, if you know what I mean."

"Bow chica wow wow."

Time to make my exit. I walk away as fast as I can while not actually breaking out into a run. But no matter how fast I move, I can't escape the sound of my sisters' laughing behind me. Laugh away, little sisters. Laugh away. Revenge will be mine.

Chapter 6

Jealousy – an emotion that causes you to do extremely stupid things e.g., drink tequila shots

LYRIC

I enter the *Electric Vibes* bar on Friday night and just like every other time I enter, it feels as if I've stepped back in time to the 1960s. Or is it 1970s? Either way, this bar is a folk and psychedelic rock hippie haven.

The walls are covered in posters and other paraphernalia from the peak of the hippie revolution. There isn't a matching chair in the place and colored lights decorate the walls and ceiling, which makes for a unique experience after a few too many beers.

"Everybody hide! It's the po-po," the owner, Lennon, yells the same as he does every single time I've entered this bar since I was elected Chief of Police whether I'm in uniform or not.

"Off duty tonight, Lennon," I tell him.

Lennon isn't his real name. He re-named himself Lennon when he relocated to Winter Falls two decades ago. I doubt he remembers what his real name is anymore. He's the poster child for why even Winter Falls doesn't tolerate hard drug usage.

My brothers, Phoenix and River, wave me over to their table. River pours me a beer from the pitcher on the table, and I drink half of the glass down in one go.

"Long week?" River asks.

Phoenix snorts. "I bet it was a tough week on poor Chief Alston what with every single lady in town bringing him a casserole this week."

I wish he was joking, but he's not. When the local grapevine found out Aspen was back in town for an extended visit, every unattached woman from the age of eighteen to fifty decided to step up their bid to tie me down.

"I should shut down the Facebook group," I mutter.

The Facebook group is how the grapevine manages to disseminate gossip to the entire town in mere seconds.

Phoenix chuckles. "They'd come after you with pitchforks if you tried."

"Pitchforks? He should be so lucky. They'd stage a sit-in at the police station, and man, can the people of this town can hold a sit-in to end all sit-ins."

River isn't wrong. When I was considering giving a gas company permission to have a gas station within town limits, the uproar was unbelievable. Needless to say, the gas station is beyond city limits. It didn't matter how much I argued about the waste of fuel to drive to the gas station, it was a waste of my breath.

"What are you going to do?" Phoenix asks.

I finish my beer before responding. "About what?" I have a sneaking suspicion I know what.

"About Aspen and how you've never gotten over her."

"If I wanted to sit around and talk about my feelings, I would have gone to Mom and Dad's house," I grumble.

"Too bad for you they're on a trip to discover themselves in Bali." River chuckles.

"Don't pretend you're not used to deep diving into your feelings," Phoenix adds. "You were raised by hippies in a hippie town, and you choose to stay here. In fact, as I remember it, you refused to even discuss leaving with Aspen."

"Bull-headed," River grunts under his breath.

Phoenix wiggles his eyebrows. "I know what I'd do if the woman I've been in love with since tenth grade returned to town."

"Who says I'm still in love with her?"

"Does he think we're stupid?" River asks Phoenix as if I'm not sitting right here.

Phoenix shrugs. "He's probably power hungry after spending a week fighting off the single women of Winter Falls."

"Whatever," I grumble. "Who wants another pitcher of beer?"

There's no worrying about drinking and driving in Winter Falls. If I don't want to stumble the few blocks home, I can grab a free bike. There are several strategically located outside of the bar. After the golf cart slash drinking slash polo game got out of hand last year, the police department stepped in to encourage residents to bike after drinking, and by encourage, I mean the rental golf carts mysteriously disappear after 9 p.m.

"Guess who happens to stroll into the bar right when Lyric offers to buy us a refill?"

I follow River's gaze and watch as the West sisters saunter into the bar. Their entrance does not go unnoticed by the rest of the crowd. Every heterosexual male in the place turns to ogle them as they swagger inside.

"Aspen!" Lennon rushes out from behind the bar to greet her. He lifts her up to twirl her around.

She giggles and slaps at his shoulders. "Let me down, you big Beatles loving oaf."

"Don't make fun of the greatest rock band in history."

"I thought the greatest rock band in history was The Doors."

"Much you have to learn, Cloud."

She sticks her tongue out at him. She hates it when people call her by her middle name.

"At least tell me you still make those delicious pitchers of margaritas."

I groan. Aspen and margaritas is a bad idea. "The last time you drank one of those pitchers you ended up streaking through downtown."

She stiffens upon hearing my voice before turning around to wink at me. "Good thing someone reminded me last week how public nudity is not illegal in this town."

Her sister, Ellery, pats my arm. "Don't worry, Chief. She's sharing with us."

Does she think her words are some kind of comfort? All five West sisters drinking is a recipe for disaster.

"Maybe I should go change back into my uniform."

"Why?" Lilac asks. "Do you prefer to role play in bed?"

I wish I could say she's teasing. She's not. This is Lilac. Her big, scientific brain never switches off – until the margaritas are drunk. One of those and she's as bad as her sisters.

"Let them have their fun, po-po." Lennon sets a pitcher of frozen strawberry margaritas on the bar.

I point at him. "Don't come crying to me when the riots begin."

He cocks an eyebrow at me. "When have I ever come crying to you?"

He hasn't. He's probably the only bar owner in the world who lets his customers duke it out inside his establishment. Although, there isn't much fighting in a town full of hippies. Unless they're discussing which songs belong to the psychedelic rock genre. Then, fists can and will be involved. There's a reason I've tried banning quiz night at the bar.

Aspen glances over her shoulder at me and, while staring straight into my eyes, orders, "A round of tequila shots, barkeep."

I rub a hand over my face. This night will not end well.

Ashlyn hip checks me. "Maybe give her a break. She needs to let loose. Her entire life was destroyed in a fire."

At her words, my gaze strays to Aspen's forearms. She's wearing another long-sleeved shirt despite the temperature hitting the high-80s today.

"Don't give me a reason to regret this."

"Me?" She bats her eyelashes at me.

I narrow my eyes on her. "Are you even old enough to be in here?"

She sticks her hand in my face. "And now we're done."

Aspen hands me a tequila shot. "Come on, Mr. Fuddy Duddy. For old time's sake."

She knows I hate tequila. I lift my glass. "For old time's sake."

I down my shot as Aspen grimaces her way through hers. "Why do you drink it if you don't enjoy the taste?"

"Because it makes me feel good!"

"And you look good, too, baby."

I whip my head around to glare at whoever said those words. It's an out-of-towner. Of course, it is. No one else would dare comment on my woman. Hold up. *My* woman. Aspen is not my woman, and she hasn't been in a long ass time. She made damn sure of it when she left me in the dust after she hightailed it out of town.

I step away from her. "Have a good night."

She beams up at me. "You too, Chief."

I grab a fresh pitcher of beer and return to my brothers.

"Ten bucks says he gets in a fist fight before we finish this pitcher," River says.

Phoenix shakes his hand. "You're on."

"I'm not getting into a fist fight."

"Oh yeah?" River points across the room to where Aspen is dancing. She's surrounded by men. And those men not trying to dance with her have their eyes glued to her ass.

My hands fist and my heart squeezes as jealousy seizes me, but I'm not allowed to be jealous. Aspen and I were over a decade ago when she abandoned me. I force my hands to loosen and grip my beer mug.

"It's fine. She's not my business. She can do whatever she wants."

River and Phoenix burst out laughing. They slap the table and roar. At least everyone in the bar is now staring at us instead of Aspen.

The song ends and Lennon moseys to the stage. "It's time for karaoke."

Good. No one dances to karaoke. Although you never know what the West sisters will do.

Aspen jumps up and down with her hand raised. "Me first. Me first."

"Up first is our very own Aspen Cloud back home from the wilds of Dallas."

Everyone claps as Aspen jumps on stage and whispers the song she wants to sing in his ear. He nods and hands her the microphone. I hear the distinctive keyboard intro of the music and swear under my breath. She wouldn't. Her gaze lands on me and she winks. She would.

Light My Fire is our song. The song was playing when we both lost our virginity while making love at the falls. Except for the location and the choice of song, our first time was cliché to the nth degree – candles, music, chocolate-covered strawberries. It was perfect. Aspen knows exactly how I feel about this song.

"Uh oh." River blocks my movement. I didn't even realize I was standing, let alone moving toward the stage.

Phoenix grasps my shoulder. "Come on, Lyric. Let's get out of here."

"Yeah, bro. The old guard is playing poker tonight. Let's go relieve them of their money."

"I don't want to play poker," I grit out.

"Yeah, well, I don't want to have to throw your ass in jail."

I frown at River. "I never should have deputized you."

"But you did." He grins as he shoves me toward the exit.

I glance over my shoulder at Aspen one more time before we leave, but Phoenix is blocking my view.

"Unless you're ready to deal with the fallout, let it go, bro. Let it go."

He's right. I can hardly act like a jealous gorilla over a woman I haven't claimed as my own. And I won't be claiming her. The woman deserted me. I can't forgive her for ghosting me the way she did. And if I can't forgive her, we don't stand a chance of surviving as a couple.

Chapter 7

Toilets – not as self-explanatory as you'd think

I GAG WHEN I lift the lid on the toilet. Why did I agree to help Ellery clean this morning? Oh yeah. She made her agreement to go out with us last night contingent on my promise to help her clean rooms this morning. Not my best plan. Especially considering the number of margaritas I drank last night. Tequila is not my friend.

"If you're going to throw up in the toilet, don't forget to clean it afterwards," Ellery orders from the guest room where she's changing the sheets.

"I hate you," I mutter.

Of course, she hears me. Ms. I Don't Get Hangovers apparently also has perfect hearing.

"I love you, too," she sings.

I decide it's time for a break before I do end up throwing up in the toilet. I collapse on a chair in the bedroom and watch as she fluffs the pillows. "Why are we cleaning anyway? Don't you have staff for this?"

"I wish." She snorts. "Do you realize how hard it is to find cleaning staff to work on the weekends in a small town during the summer?"

"I'm guessing by the sarcasm it's not easy." Unlike my sister Lilac, who can sometimes be confused with an emotionless robot, I can detect sarcasm.

"The real problem is turnover. Twenty rooms are not a whole lot, but it's too many for one person to clean when all the rooms check out late and every new arrival wants an early check-in."

"Why don't you implement a minimum two-day stay? Or have a reduced special weekend rate? I bet the money you'd lose on the price would be made up by what you save in cleaning costs."

"I've done the calculations. The numbers are not in my favor."

"What about doing weekend deals with a bit extra? I bet the new brewery in town would contribute to a welcome to Winter Falls package." I snap my fingers. "In fact, you could make a basket with all of the unique gifts the town has to offer."

"You may be on to something. I'll talk to the other business owners at the next chamber of commerce meeting." She collapses on the chair next to me. "You should come to the next meeting."

My brow wrinkles. "Why? I'm not a business owner in Winter Falls."

"Oh yeah, I forgot. You 'live' in Dallas."

"What's with the air quotes? I do live in Dallas. I'm in town temporarily."

"Sure, you are." She stands and slaps my thigh. "Enough lollygagging. The toilet isn't going to clean itself."

I manage to finish cleaning the toilet without losing my breakfast – probably because I haven't managed to actually eat anything yet today – and move on to cleaning the vanity. I open the drawer next to the sink and scream.

Ellery rushes into the room. "What is it? Please don't be a rat. Please don't be a rat."

My nose wrinkles. "Do you have rats?" Ew. Those beady eyes and long tails freak me out. "Never mind. In there." I point to the drawer.

"Yuck! Why did you show me a used condom? Gross."

"If I had to see it, so did you. Now, get rid of it."

She steps back while holding up her hands. "Nuh-uh. You found it. You deal with it." She scurries back to the bedroom before I can grab her.

"I am never asking you out for sisters' night out ever again!" I yell after her retreating form.

I wrap my gloved hand in toilet paper before removing the condom and throwing it in the trash. "People are pigs. How much more difficult would it have been to put the condom in the trash as opposed to the drawer? What could possibly possess a person to think a used condom belongs in a drawer? What's wrong with flushing it down the toilet?"

"Not in my B&B," Ellery shouts.

"Do you have bat hearing or something? Lilac should do experiments on you."

She sticks her head in the bathroom. "You do know Lilac's an environmental engineer and not a biologist."

I do the mature thing. I stick my tongue out at her.

"If you're done dillydallying, we've got another five rooms to go."

"First, I was lollygagging, and now I'm dillydallying. Since when do you talk like Grandma?"

She chuckles. "As if Babushka would ever be caught saying those words."

"True."

Dad's mother, who thankfully doesn't live in Winter Falls, prefers to speak in broken English with a thick Russian accent despite speaking fluent English. She loves to lay the Russian immigrant act on thick despite having lived in the US for sixty years now and having been an English teacher in the Soviet Union before then.

I grab my cleaning supplies and follow Ellery to the next room we need to clean.

"Why do I have to clean the bathrooms? Why can't I do the bedding?"

"If you do this bathroom, I'll do the next three," she offers.

Works for me. Two bathrooms for me and three for her. Win for me.

I clean the bathtub before moving onto the sink and vanity. I step as far away from the vanity as possible and use one finger to open the drawer before peeking inside. Phew. No used condom. I finish cleaning the sink and vanity before approaching the toilet.

I give myself a pep talk. I can do this. When I bought the building where my bookstore is located, the place was a complete dump. To save cost, I did all of the demolition work myself. The things I saw in the toilet and kitchen area. Shiver. I got this.

I finish scrubbing the toilet, but when I push the handle to flush, nothing happens. "Sis, I think the toilet's broken."

"Jiggle the handle."

I jiggle the handle and try again. Water pours into the toilet, but it doesn't drain. I jump away before the bowl overflows, but then I remember – it won't overflow. All toilets in Winter Falls are low-flow water conserving. Duh.

"Sis. I think it's stopped up."

"There's a plunger on the cleaning cart."

"Shouldn't you handle this?"

She laughs. "Nope."

I stomp to the cart and find the plunger.

"You are seriously uninvited to all sisters' nights out this year. No, this decade. No, until the end of time."

"Yeah, yeah, whatever. You'll be back begging for me to be your wing woman in no time."

"You are the worst wing woman ever! You let me sing *Light My Fire*."

"What did you expect me to do? Tackle you off the stage?"

"Hell yeah! Whatever it took to keep me from singing that song."

My stomach clenches as I remember the expression on Lyric's face as his brothers dragged him out of the bar last night. The betrayal there was easy to read. I'm such an idiot. What did I think I was doing? Did I expect him to get down on his knees and apologize for cheating on me? It hasn't happened for the last decade, it's not going to happen now.

"Got it. Tackle Aspen off the stage should she dare sing a Doors sing during karaoke. Check."

"I know you're being sarcastic, and I do not approve."

"What are you? The sarcasm police? Do you and Lilac have matching sarcasm police uniforms?" She points to the bathroom. "Now, get your butt moving. We have four more rooms to clean after this."

I make my way to the bathroom. Not because I'm following orders, but because I want to get these four rooms done so I can return to my bed to die with some dignity like any normal person with a hangover on Saturday morning.

I lift the plunger, intent on placing it in the toilet bowl when I notice something red in the water. What is that? I tug my gloves up until they're covering me from my fingers to my elbows before dipping my hand in. I catch hold of something and pull. It doesn't budge, so I pull harder – to no avail. I grunt and pull as hard as I can. The item gives way and I fly through the air before hitting the wall and landing flat on my ass. Ow. I lift my hand to discover the item clogging the toilet was a pair of red underwear. A pair of red, granny pants to be exact.

"Look what was clogging the toilet."

Ellery doesn't look. "I don't want to know."

"You do. Trust me. You do."

"If you show me a giant turd, I'm going to kick your ass."

"Not a turd, I promise."

She glances over her shoulder. "A pair of underwear?"

"Yep. Red, granny pants to be exact."

"I'm all for granny pants, especially when it's that time of month, but in my toilet? Not okay."

I throw the pair into the trash. "I hope she doesn't call wondering where her panties are."

Ellery smooths out the comforter. "Done."

We move onto the next room, and I fling the door open. "You have to clean the toilet this time," I sing.

She snatches the supplies out of my hands with a roll of her eyes. "As if I haven't cleaned more toilets than you'll even use in your entire life."

"Challenge accepted!"

I giggle as I fling back the comforter. But when I notice what's right there in the middle of the bed, I scream.

"Nope! I'm done. Feel free to tell everyone I break my promises," I say as I back away from the bed with my hand over my nose and mouth.

"What's wrong now, Drama Empress?"

I point to the turd laying on the bed. "Not a drama queen."

"Shit."

"Literally." A giggle escapes, and I slap a hand over my mouth to stop myself from falling into hysterics.

"Maybe I should include adult diapers in the welcome package."

There's no chance I can stop my laughter now. I laugh until my tummy aches before collapsing in a chair.

"I'm glad you're home," Ellery says as she sits in the chair next to me.

I squeeze her arm. "Me too."

The reason I'm home sucks, but I refuse to think about my poor business right now. There's plenty of time for feeling sorry for myself later when I'm alone in bed in my childhood bedroom. It's easy to feel pathetic in a room with the walls still decorated like they were when I was sixteen and obsessed with boy bands.

Chapter 8

Stick your foot in your mouth – act like a total idiot and say the most stupid thing ever

LYRIC

"Hi, Chief Alston."

I look up from my desk to discover Love Hill standing in my office doorway. She's wearing a bikini top and cut-off shorts while holding a box of donuts. Love's breasts are barely restrained in her bikini top, and I bet if she turns around her butt cheeks will be peeking out of her shorts. Sometimes I wish there was a town ordinance about public decency.

"What can I do for you, Ms. Hill?"

She approaches the desk and leans over to set the donuts in front of me. My body has no reaction to her shoving her chest in front of my face. It's more interested in a girl with crazy curly hair wearing long-sleeved t-shirts to hide burns the whole town knows about anyway.

"I thought you might be hungry."

The single, female population is suddenly incredibly concerned with my eating habits. Funny how this concern coincides with the return to town of one Aspen Cloud West.

"Thanks."

When I don't say anything more, she bats her fake eyelashes at me. I may be a man, but it's hard to miss how those things attached to her eyes are fake. Too bad for her I prefer fresh-faced women.

"I thought maybe you might want to get a bite to eat with me this evening."

I bite back my growl at her words. I'm no stranger to women asking me out. I'm one of the few eligible bachelors in town after all. But it's a constant thing these days.

"I'm good. Thanks."

She juts out her bottom lip in a pout. I nearly roll my eyes. Pouty women have no effect on me. Sarcastic women on the other hand— I need to stop thinking about Aspen. She's obviously not harboring any feelings for me. Not to mention, I can't trust her to stick around.

I shift the donut box off of my files. "If you'll excuse me, I need to get back to work."

"Of course, Chief," she says but doesn't leave.

I nod toward the door. "Can you see yourself out? I really do need to get some work done."

Her shoulders slump, but she spins around and stomps off. I wait until I hear the front door to the station close before I move.

I dump the box of donuts on Sage's desk. Sage is the glue holding our small police department together. She's the office manager, my personal assistant, and the dispatcher all rolled into one. She's also a pain in my ass.

"Why do you let her back into my office?"

Sage shrugs her shoulders. "I'm hungry for donuts."

"It had nothing at all to do with the bet you have going with the office about which woman I ask out first?"

I'm not blind. I know the office is betting on my dating life. Hell, if I weren't the one being pursued by the women of this town who are suddenly acting like they're grizzly bears chasing down a baby deer, I'd get it on the action.

She widens her eyes and clutches her non-existent pearls. "Why Chief Alston, would I ever do such a thing?"

I snort. "You babysat me and changed my diapers. You are not some young, innocent thing."

She ignores me and opens the box of donuts. "Who's hungry?"

The two police officers on dayshift, Peace and Freedom, sprint to her desk. If I hadn't seen them at the diner this morning scarfing down breakfast, I would think they hadn't eaten in months with as fast they move.

Peace picks up a donut, takes a bite, and sighs. "Rowan makes the best strawberry filled donuts in the world."

"Who knew natural and organic could taste this good?" Freedom groans around his bite.

I don't know why Freedom is surprised by how good natural and organic tastes. Any food you buy in this town is natural and made with local ingredients. It's one of the reasons tourists flock here. And all of the food is mouth-watering delicious. Those chain donut stores I tried while in college can't compare.

"I'm going to do some rounds," I say before leaving.

"Say hi to Aspen from me!" Sage yells after me.

"I'm not going to visit Aspen!" Great. Now, I'm whining like a snotty teenager.

I descend the steps of the courthouse slash city hall slash police department and turn left. Since the temperatures are in the eighties today, Main Street is deserted. Most residents can be found at the river in this type of weather.

I stroll to the end of Main Street and cross the street before turning back toward the town square. The heat feels oppressive. At least my uniform doesn't include body armor. In a town where the residents staged a sit-in when the police department changed the policy to allow officers to carry weapons, there isn't much need for body armor.

I'm contemplating stopping at *Feather's Frozen Delights* for an ice cream cone when I notice there's another person rambling through town. I grin when I realize it's Aspen. The grin drops from my face when I note what she's doing.

"Aspen West, I'm going to have to write you a citation."

She startles from her hunched over position where she's picking up dog poop and ends up falling on her ass.

She glares up at me. "What's with the booming voice, Lyric? Were you trying to scare me to death?"

Her dog, named Waffles of all things, barks and comes to stand next to her. She scratches him behind his ears. "It's okay, boy. This guy is all bark and no bite."

"Actually." I point to the bag of dog poop she dropped. "You're violating town ordinance."

Her nose scrunches. "I am? I thought picking up my dog's poop was a good thing. What do you want me to do? Leave it there for some kid to slip on."

I hold out my hand. She stares at it for a few seconds before sighing and allowing me to help her to her feet.

She brushes the grass off of her butt, and I don't bother to avert my eyes. The view reminds me of how fantastic her ass feels in my hands.

"Well?" she says and brings me out of my fond memories of her naked body. When I merely stare at her since I lost track of our conversation, she continues, "What did I do wrong this time?"

I clear my throat and point to the plastic bag her dog poop is in. "As you are aware, plastic is outlawed in town."

She rolls her eyes. "Yes, I know. But how else am I going to dispose of Waffle's waste? The bag is biodegradable, and I'm planning to throw it in the composting bin exclusive for dog waste."

I frown. She really is trying to do the right thing. If I cite her now, I'll never hear the end of it.

"I'll let you go this one time." When she tries to speak, I hold up a hand to stop her. "Hear me out. But you can't use those plastic bags again. Stop by Forest's pet store. He has plant-based biobags."

She looks down at Waffles. "Did you hear the police officer, baby? You're going to cost me a fortune."

I cringe. The whole reason Aspen's staying in town is because she's out of money and the insurance company is dragging its feet. But if I tell her Forest will give her a box of biobags for free, she'll think we pity her. She never did learn the difference between pity and a neighbor lending a helping hand.

I kneel down and stick my hand out at Waffles. "Hey, boy."

He waits until Aspen nods her approval before sniffing my hand. I must pass his sniff inspection since he wags his tail and starts licking my hand. I chuckle and push him off me.

"What kind of dog is he?"

"The near as the vet can tell he's a mix between a beagle and some type of shepherd."

The dog rolls to his back and I rub his belly for a while before standing.

"Do you have some water for him? It's hot out here today."

"We stopped at *Unleashed* for some refreshment."

I notice her face is flushed and there's sweat on her brow. "Speaking of how hot it is, why are you wearing another long-sleeved shirt?"

She glares at me. "You know why."

"Everyone in town knows about the burns. There's no reason to hide them or be ashamed."

She rears back. "You think I'm ashamed? I ran into a burning building to try and save the business I spent the past decade building. I'm not ashamed of my actions."

My jaw clenches. "You ran into a burning building?" What was she thinking? I could have lost her.

"I was thinking my entire life was going up in flames."

"Are you out of your mind? You're not flame resistant."

"Yeah." She nods to her arms. "I kind of figured that out."

"Not again, Aspen. Promise me you won't go running willy-nilly into a fire again."

"Why would I promise you anything of the sort? You're nothing to me. You're just a big, fat cheater who acts as if he's the one who was done wrong."

"What? I'm not a cheater. What are you talking about?" I'm not talking smack. I seriously have no idea what she's talking about.

She rolls her eyes. "Whatever. Continue to pretend I don't know about it. It's fine. I'm used to it." She picks up the dog leash. "Come on, Waffles. Time to get you home."

I grasp her shoulder and she growls at me. "You should know better than to touch a woman without her permission, Chief Alston."

As soon as I drop my hand, she scurries away. What the hell is she talking about? I never cheated on Aspen. Only a fool would cheat on the woman he loves. And I'm no fool.

What I am is confused. I need to get to the bottom of this misunderstanding because I have a feeling whatever this is, is standing in the way of any reunion I hope to have with Aspen.

Yeah, I said reunion. I might as well stop lying to myself now. I want Aspen. I never stopped wanting her. Can I get over how she abandoned me? I don't know, but I have to at least try.

Chapter 9

Trickster – someone who uses all of her mom skills to get her daughter to do what she wants her to

I FLIP OVER IN bed to check the time on the clock. 10 a.m. I'm usually up by 7 a.m. back in Dallas, but I have no reason to get out of bed now. What is there for me to do here in Winter Falls besides stare at the walls while wondering why my insurance company hates me so? No thanks. I roll over intent on going back to sleep.

Knock. Knock. Knock.

"Aspen! Time to get up, lazy bones."

I groan. "Go away!"

The sheet is ripped away from me. "Get up," Mom orders.

"Why? What do I have to do today anyway?" I know I'm whining, but I can't seem to stop myself. I blame my childhood bedroom. Teenage hormones must have invaded my subconscious via the walls while I was sleeping.

"Stop feeling sorry for yourself."

"Am I not allowed to feel sorry for myself? My entire life is shit. My business burned down. My home above the bookstore burned down. The café next door I invested all of my savings in burned down. And." I pause for dramatic effect. "The insurance company thinks I'm an arsonist!"

She rolls her eyes. "The insurance company doesn't think you committed arson. They're using it as an excuse to drag out the time until they have to pay out. Your dad thinks they'll offer you a settlement for half of the amount."

I shoot to my feet. "They better not! I pay those overpriced premiums on time every damn month. They owe me!"

"Good. You're up."

I narrow my eyes on her. My mom is the trickiest person in the world. And she's gotten worse since she became principal of the local school.

I plop back down on the bed. "Oh no, you don't." She grasps my hand and tries to tug me to my feet. I don't let her.

"I need you to run to Saffron's house. I made her an apple pie."

"Why would Saffron be home now? Doesn't she need to be in the bookstore?"

Saffron has owned the local bookstore, *Fall into a Good Book*, for as long as I can remember.

"She broke her hip last week. She got home from the hospital yesterday."

"Poor Saffron, but can't you take her the pie yourself?"

It's hot outside and putting on another long-sleeved shirt sounds like absolute torture.

Mom sighs before sitting beside me on the bed. "Your burns are practically healed," she says proving mothers have perfected mind-reading. "There's no need to cover them up anymore."

I study my forearms. They're red and a bit swollen, but otherwise healing up nicely. "I know, but the doctor says I need to cover them up for at least another week."

She stands before I have a chance to respond. "I have a light cover-up you can wear outside to protect you from the sun. I'll get it while you have your shower and get dressed." She stops at the door. "And maybe clean up your room a bit, too."

Dissent is futile. I drag myself to the bathroom to shower. Once I'm ready for the day, I enter the kitchen to find Mom waiting for me. She thrusts a pie into my hands before I can even grab a cup of coffee.

"Can't I have breakfast first?" My stomach rumbles.

"If you wanted breakfast, you should have gotten up before ten."

I don't bother arguing. When Mom's mind is set, it's set. Besides, Saffron will share this pie with me.

"And don't be eating Saffron's pie," Mom warns.

What she doesn't know, won't hurt her.

I stroll the two blocks to Saffron's house. Winter Falls is lined up in a grid pattern. Main Street extends north and south down the middle of town with several streets to the west and east. The farmers live further out of the city, but otherwise, everyone in the entire town lives within a mile of Main Street. It's what makes using bikes and golf carts for travel so easy.

"Come in," Saffron shouts in response to my knock on the door.

I enter her house to find her sitting in a recliner in the middle of the living room.

"Aspen Cloud." She smiles in recognition. "Please tell me your momma sent an apple pie over."

"She did. Shall I make some coffee and slice us two pieces?"

"You read my mind, child."

We eat our pie without talking. Mom's pie is too good to ruin with blabbing or gossiping, which is the favorite pastime of everyone in this town.

"What were you doing to break your hip?" I ask after I collect the plates and pour more coffee.

"Trying to move some boxes of books I ordered."

"Saffron! You shouldn't be moving boxes of books on your own."

She sighs. "Who else is going to do it?"

"Don't you have any help?" When I was in high school, I helped out at the bookstore a few hours a week. Why isn't some other high school student helping her now?

She frowns. "Business hasn't exactly been going very well lately. You know how hard it is to keep a bookstore afloat in these digital times."

I do. It's one of the reasons I purchased the café next door to my bookstore. I had a coffee corner in my store, but it wasn't big enough for customers to have a drink or pastry while browsing or reading.

"I'm sorry."

"Oh!" Her eyes widen and she feigns surprise. I narrow my gaze on her. I'm not buying her act.

"What is it?"

"Why don't you help me out in the store while you're home?"

"I—"

"Just until my hip heals."

I guess if it's for a week, I could help. "How long did the doctor say you needed to say off your feet?"

"At least four weeks, maybe eight."

"I don't know how long I'll be in town for. As soon as my insurance payout hits my bank account, I'm leaving." I have a lot of rebuilding to do, and I want the store open before the Christmas season hits.

She waves a hand in dismissal. "You can work at the store until you leave."

I bite my lip. "I don't know."

"It's going to sit there closed otherwise. And this is prime tourist season."

"I thought I'd give myself a little break while I'm here." I glance at my arms.

"Those burns are healing up nicely." She pauses. "Besides, weren't you complaining a minute ago about not having anything to do?"

There's only one place she could have found out about my whining. I glare at her. "Mom phoned you, didn't she?"

"Don't get mad at Ruby. It was my idea."

It's my prerogative as a daughter to get mad at my mom whether my anger is founded or not.

"What's holding you back?"

Good question. I love *Fall Into A Good Book*. The bookstore is where my love of reading began. I used to spend hours on the window seat reading to my heart's content. When the guidance counselor in high school asked me what I wanted to be when I grew up, I couldn't shout bookstore owner fast enough.

Writing the 'Great American Novel' would have been my preference if I had an ounce of talent. But I don't. Some people are writers, and some are readers. I fall into the later category. And I've made my peace with it.

I've more than made my peace with it actually. I love the creativity necessary to keep a brick-and-mortar business thriving in this day and age when people prefer to buy everything from books to groceries online.

So, what's holding me back from accepting Saffron's offer? One word – control.

"You have to give me complete control to organize events and change the store in any way I want."

"Granted."

I narrow my eyes on her. She answered awful quick.

"I'm serious. I may decide to get rid of the entire sci-fi section." I wouldn't. The very idea is sacrilege.

"Whatever you want is fine, dear."

"And I will leave when my insurance claim pays out."

"I understand. The small town of Winter Falls can't keep the attention of an adventurer such as yourself. Not even when Lyric Alston is the Chief of Police."

I ignore the comment about Lyric. I'm used to the town not understanding Lyric and I are finished.

"Okay. You have a deal." I hold out my hand and we shake on it.

"Welcome aboard." She nods to a set of keys on the coffee table. "Those are the keys."

How convenient to have the keys ready and waiting for me. "A bit presumptuous of you."

"I was hopeful is all."

Whatever. "Who wants another piece of pie?"

While we eat, she tells me more about the store. Based on what she's saying, I have my work cut out for me. She doesn't have any inventory software and she uses some free software program for her bookkeeping. My time in Winter Falls suddenly got a whole lot busier.

"I'm off," I say once I finish the dishes and put the pie away. "Unless you need something else from me."

"I'm good. Petal's stopping by with lunch in an hour."

Small town living at its best. Everyone bands together to help each other out. Saffron will have lunch and dinner delivered until she can manage on her own.

I kiss her cheek before leaving. I've barely stepped onto the porch when I hear her pick up the phone. I pause. I'm not exactly eavesdropping. I need to re-tie my shoe is all.

"Operation Weston is a go," I hear her say into the phone.

Weston? What does Weston mean? I gasp when I realize it's a portmanteau of two last names. To be specific, Aspen West and Lyric Alston. West plus Alston equals Weston. I've been had.

But the people of this town are wrong if they think they can coerce me into staying here. My life isn't here. It's in Dallas. No matter how much I love this town and the people in it, I won't stay.

My heart contracts at the idea of leaving, but I ignore it. I got over my homesickness once. I can do it again.

Chapter 10

Fine – a word that causes terror in a male regardless of the species

LYRIC

I kick my boots off as I enter my house. It's been a long ass day. On top of the temps hitting the high nineties – never fun when you're wearing a uniform – the tourists were testing my last nerve today.

I know the businesses of Winter Falls rely on tourism to survive, but tourists often don't 'get' the town's philosophy, despite our 'green' philosophy being the whole reason for their visit in the first place.

Case in point? I spent nearly an hour arguing with a man who wanted to drive his gas guzzling truck through town. The same man who was in town because he scheduled a tour with my brother, River, to discuss green energy.

I dump my utility belt on the kitchen table and secure my pistol in my safe before digging a beer out of the refrigerator and collapsing on the sofa. But before I can switch on the television, my phone rings. I'm tempted to ignore it for a few moments, but the Chief of Police doesn't have the option of ignoring his phone.

"Chief Alston."

"Chief. It's Feather." At the tremble in her voice, I'm instantly on alert.

"What is it?"

"I think someone's breaking into the bookstore."

I stand and march to my safe. "What happened?"

"After I shut *Feather's Frozen Delights*, I was walking through the alleyway on my way home, and I saw there was a light on at *Fall Into A Good Book*."

"And it wasn't Saffron?" I ask as I open my safe and remove my gun.

"You know as well as me Saffron's laid up with her hip."

Damn. I hope some tourist didn't notice the bookstore was empty and decide the place is easy pickings.

"Don't worry, Feather. I'll check it out."

"Thank you, Lyric." She hangs up before I have a chance to respond.

Weird. Normally, I can't get the people of this town to shut up. She must be really worried about the bookstore. Crime is always upsetting, but in a town with an extremely low crime rate such as Winter Falls, it's extra upsetting.

I secure my weapon to my hip and shove my feet into my boots before jumping in my golf cart and driving toward Main Street.

I stop the cart a few stores away from the bookstore so as to not alert anyone in the store of my presence. I survey the area as I make my way to the bookstore. Main Street is locked up tight.

Except for the brewery, the diner, and the bar, the businesses of the town are closed by six p.m.

I don't notice any lights on in the bookstore from the street, so I decide to circle around the building to the back alley.

When I turn the corner, I notice the backdoor of the bookstore is open and light is flooding out. Damn. Looks like we have a burglar. I remove my gun and creep toward the entrance. I take a deep breath before rushing through the back door with my weapon raised to find someone leaning over a box and removing its contents.

"Police. Raise your hands and don't make any sudden movements."

"Which one is it? Raise my hands or don't make any sudden movements? I can't do both."

Shit. I know that sarcastic voice. I holster my weapon. "What are you doing in here, Aspen?"

She stands and turns around. She's wearing a skintight tank top and a tiny pair of shorts. I busy myself with my weapon to buy myself some time to get my body under control and not react to the vision of her dressed in barely decent clothes. Although, decent is a fluid word in this town.

I clear my throat. "Someone reported a disturbance."

She snorts. "Reported a disturbance? Who? The whole town knows I'm helping Saffron out while she heals. Who could have possibly called you?"

"Feather."

Her eyes widen. "Feather? The woman who stopped by on her way home to ask if I needed any help? That Feather?"

I rub a hand down my face. "I've been had."

"Stupid Project Weston," she mumbles.

"Project Weston? What are you talking about?"

She pauses and I think she isn't going to answer me, but after a moment, she sighs and explains. "I think Project Weston is the code name the town gave to this cockamamie idea of getting the two of us back together."

I cough to hide my smile at the idea. The whole town wants us back together? Yet another reason I love this town and never wanted to leave. But I know better than to let Aspen know how I feel about the idea.

"You're helping Saffron out? I thought you were leaving town as soon as you can."

She goes back to emptying the box. "I am, but Saffron tricked me into helping out."

I snatch the books from her. "Where do you want these?"

She points to a table. "Over there."

"How did Saffron trick you?"

"She gave me this boo-hoo story of how bad things are with the bookstore and how she doesn't have anyone to help her, but she probably made the whole thing up."

I think back over the past months. Has Saffron's business been suffering?

"Actually, the bookstore hasn't been open much over the past few months."

She stops emptying the box to raise an eyebrow at me. "You're serious?"

"It's easy enough to figure out, assuming Saffron gave you access to her accounting books."

"She did, but I don't know about easy. Saffron and accounting aren't the best of friends. When I asked her what accounting software she uses, she said, and I quote here 'the free one'. No idea what the name of it is. And, get this, she does her own taxes." She throws her hands in the air. "Who does their own taxes?"

"I do my own taxes."

"Of course, Mr. Goody Two Shoes does his own taxes."

"Hey now. I'm the Chief of Police, not an innocent little girl."

She knows damn well I'm no Goody Two Shoes. My early years before I joined the police force were not beyond reproach. She's an eyewitness to the majority of the shenanigans I pulled.

She waves away my irritation. "I meant you're not a business owner. No business owner should do their own taxes. It's sacrilege."

I cross my arms over my chest and watch as her gaze zeroes in on my biceps. I flex them and her tongue peeks out to lick her lips. Oh yeah. Someone's still affected by my body. Even if she doesn't want to be.

"You've been away too long. The only thing sacrilege in Winter Falls is abusing the environment. Any other bad behavior is open to interpretation."

"I don't know. The townspeople were pretty irritated with us when we removed all the batteries from their golf carts."

"It was the night before the Fourth of July parade. The parade was delayed for over an hour while you sent the entire town on a wild goose chase to find the batteries."

She shrugs. "What did they expect to happen when they voted Love Hill to be the parade queen instead of me?"

"No one expected you to get mad about it. Especially since you held a sit-in the year before to end the whole parade king and queen business."

She huffs. "They still shouldn't have voted for Love Hill and you. She gloated for a week about how she was going to steal you away from me."

I step close to her. "And yet, she didn't."

Her eyes narrow. "Sure, she didn't."

My brow furrows. This isn't the first time she's referred to me being with another woman while we were together. "What's with the cryptic comments?"

She shoves me away. "I didn't give you permission to be in my personal space, Chief."

She can push me away all she wants, but I am getting to the bottom of this. She's questioned me one too many times.

"What are you talking about? The other day you claimed I was a cheater and now you're insinuating Love Hill stole me away from you. What's going on?"

Instead of answering me, she opens up another box. I slam the top closed.

"Answer my question."

She glares at me. "Is that an order, Chief Alston?"

"Don't push me, Aspen."

She holds my gaze for several long moments, and I think she's finally going to tell me what's crawled up her butt. But she doesn't. Not my stubborn girl.

"It's ancient history, Lyric. Just leave it."

It's obviously not ancient history if she keeps bringing it up. The next thing I know she'll be telling me she's fine, which every male worth his weight knows is the red flag to end all red flags.

"Now, if you'll excuse me, I have a ton of inventory to catalog before I can shelf it, and I need to open this place up as soon as possible."

And, in case I'm unclear how her words are an obvious dismissal, she turns her back on me and walks out of the storage area.

"Don't work too late," I call after her retreating figure.

"Don't let the door hit you in the ass on your way out."

I let her go – for now – but she can't seriously think she can get rid of me this easily.

Chapter 11

Hot yoga – because bending yourself into a pretzel isn't enough of a challenge

ELLERY TUGS ON MY arm while Juniper shoves me from behind.

"I don't understand why I can't collapse on the sofa after a hard day of working like a normal person," I pout.

"You'll feel much better after yoga. I promise," Ashlyn says.

I glare at her. "Easy for you to say, baby cakes. You're a decade younger than me."

She huffs. "I'm twenty-three. I'm not a baby!"

I wrap my arm around her neck and ruffle her hair. "You'll always be my baby sister."

She shoves me off of her. "Lucky me. When are you returning to Dallas again?"

I feel my shoulders slump. "As soon as the insurance company decides I'm not an arsonist."

"How ridiculous." Lilac purses her lips. "You were literally afraid to light candles until you were a teenager. Needless to say, you didn't light the fire. I'm not impressed with the due diligence of your insurance company."

I guess a certain sister never found out about the fire I lit at school. I swear it was an accident. Really!

"Yeah, because insurance companies usually interview people's families to learn about the victim's candle fetishes."

I slap Ellery's shoulder. "I don't have a candle fetish."

"Did I hear candle fetish?" Petal asks as she joins us. "I made up a new batch of paraffin candles yesterday. They have a nice sting to them if you know what I mean."

I shiver. I don't want to know what she means. And I certainly don't want to imagine Petal, who's not a day under sixty-five, using sex candles.

"Let me know if you want to try one out with Lyric," she sings as she presses past us to open the door to *Earth Bliss,* the yoga studio.

When she opens the door, hot air blasts toward us. "Holy cow. Is Cayenne's air-conditioning broken?"

Most homes and businesses in Winter Falls don't have air-conditioning since it consumes too much energy. And Winter Falls is all about conserving energy. Being a carbon neutral town is not some gimmick made up by the town to draw tourists. It was a conscious decision to help the earth made by the first generation of town settlers.

All this means most businesses do not have air-conditioning. In fact, in order for a business to have air-conditioning, you need approval from the chamber of commerce. Approval you can only receive after drafting an energy saving plan. Currently, the town has granted two exemptions for businesses to have air-conditioners – the bakery and *Earth Bliss.*

"Cayenne's air-conditioning is not broken." Lilac appears personally affronted by the idea. Since her job as an environmental engineer helped to approve the plans to allow *Earth Bliss* to use air-conditioning, she probably is.

"We're doing hot yoga."

My mouth drops open at Ellery's declaration.

"Do you want me to have a stroke?"

"You'll be fine. Besides, the police department isn't too far away and Chief Alston is a certified paramedic. He'll save you," Juniper says with a wink.

"Although, if you're too afraid your old body can't handle hot yoga, we'll understand," Ashlyn says before nodding to Petal who's standing with a group of gray-haired women all around her age and all of whom are preparing for the hot yoga class.

I narrow my eyes on her. I can't resist a challenge from my sister. If I do, I'll never hear the end of it. Family dinners will be overtaken with talk of how big a chicken I am.

"Fine. Let's do this."

Fifteen minutes later, I'm wondering what the big deal is with being teased by my family. Better to be alive to be teased than dead from heat stroke.

I drag my sweat stained t-shirt off of me and debate ditching my shorts. And I probably would, too, but someone hasn't done any laundry in a while and ended up wearing a pair of granny pants I probably should have thrown out five years ago.

"Wake up."

Someone nudges me, and I swat at them. "Leave me here to die in peace."

"You're not dying. You're breathing, and your heart is pumping blood to your body. There are no signs of your imminent demise." Lilac and her logic.

"Fine. Help me up."

Ellery grabs my hand and drags me to my feet. I wobble a bit once I'm on my feet.

"I hope you don't think I'm ever doing this again."

She waggles her eyebrows at me. "But you haven't enjoyed the best part yet."

"What could possibly be next? Are we going to dive into Winter Falls?"

"Don't be dramatic. Swimming in cold water after performing exercise can cause a shock to your heart." Lilac's brain is an encyclopedia of facts no one cares to know.

Ellery hooks her arm through mine. "No swimming. Now we go to the bakery to have whatever today's special is."

"It completely defeats the purpose of exercising," Lilac grumbles, but everyone ignores her.

We stumble – or maybe it's just me who stumbles – down Main Street until we reach the *Bake Me Happy* bakery. As soon as we enter, I stop to enjoy the cool air and smell of delicious baked goods.

"I could die happy now."

"What is it with you and dying today?" Lilac asks. "Do we need to have an intervention? Are you having suicidal thoughts?"

"You shouldn't interpret everything a person says literally."

"Why do you say the words if you don't mean them literally? Is this the sarcastic thing again?"

I ignore her in favor of watching Rowan, the owner of *Bake Me Happy*, enter the bakery from the kitchen. Ashlyn sighs and I glance over at her. She's gawking at Rowan like he's a piece of chocolate she can't wait to devour.

I can hardly blame her. Rowan is one sexy guy. He's way over six-foot-tall with broad shoulders and a square jaw. He looks like he should be playing football and not baking delicious treats for us to eat. Probably because he used to play pro ball.

"You have a bit of something right here." I rub the corner of my mouth. "If I had to guess, I'd say it's drool, little sis."

Ashlyn glares at me, and I giggle.

"Aspen!" Rowan greets, and anger flares in Ashlyn's eyes. Huh. Little sis is jealous. This is going to be fun.

"Rowan!" He wraps me up in a hug and whirls me around.

"I heard you were back in town, but you haven't stopped by to visit me."

I roll my eyes. "I'm here now and I'm dying from hunger."

"Again with the dying," Lilac mumbles from behind me, but – being the good sister I am – I ignore her.

He steps behind the counter. "I have just the thing. My super food donut will fill you up." He scans my body. "Especially after hot yoga with Cayenne."

I tug on the hem of my soaked t-shirt. "What gave me away?"

He sets five donuts on a plate. "You're going to love this recipe. I sprinkle the top with brown sugar to give it a little extra sweet crunch."

We settle at a table near the window with our donuts and homemade juice 'guaranteed to stop muscle ache'. I don't think anything can stop the muscle ache I'm going to have tomorrow after my first yoga class in I don't know how many years. I don't exactly have time for yoga or other exercises back in Dallas.

"So," I lean close to whisper, "how long has Ashlyn had a crush on Rowan?"

"I don't have a crush on Rowan," Ashlyn grumbles in response.

"Since high school," Juniper answers, and Ashlyn slaps the donut out of her mouth. It goes flying across the table and lands at Petal's feet.

Ashlyn throws Juniper a glare before jumping to her feet and retrieving the donut. "Sorry, Petal. My hand slipped."

Petal grins. "I understand. The same thing happens to me whenever I'm in the hunky baker's presence."

Ashlyn's cheeks darken a shade, and she ducks her head before rushing back to our table.

"This town is a menace."

I ignore her comment and tease her instead. "Rowan was two years behind me in school, which makes him eight years older than you. Ooh, you're going after an old man."

"I guess you're an old woman, then. Since you're ten years older than me and all," Ashlyn volleys right back.

Ellery clears her throat. "I suggest we put Ashlyn and Rowan on the back burner. We have other more important issues to discuss."

"We do?" I scan the group, but no one seems to know what she's talking about.

"Why won't Aspen give Lyric a chance?"

"Maybe because I don't live here. Long distance relationships don't work. You of all people are proof of that."

"You have no idea how long it will be before you can return to Dallas. Why not explore the chemistry between the two of you in the meantime?"

"The idea of there being chemistry between two human beings is absurd," Lilac points out.

"You!" Ellery points at her. "If you can't add to the conversation, keep quiet."

"I am adding to the conversation."

Before Ellery can slap Lilac, I respond, "I have explored the chemistry with Lyric. In case you forgot, the whole thing ended up in heartache."

Ellery rolls her eyes. "Yeah, because you left."

"Yeah, sis," Juniper agrees. "You don't have to leave. There's nothing left for you to prove. Everyone knows Aspen Cloud West is a successful businesswoman."

"This is ridiculous. Even if I were to stay, I would never give Lyric a second chance. Not after what he did."

I slap my hand over my mouth when I realize what I said. No one knows Lyric cheated on me because I was too ashamed to tell anyone. I can't believe how wrong I was about him. I thought he loved me. False. He couldn't wait to move on when I left.

"What are you talking about?" Ellery pries my hand away from my mouth.

"Nothing," I squeak.

"Even I can tell you're lying," Lilac says. Gee, thanks, Lilac. Way to have my back.

"Sister pinky swear."

Everyone puts their hand in the middle of the table, and we link pinky fingers.

I use my hold on their pinkies to draw them close and whisper, "Lyric cheated on me."

If I was expecting sympathy, I have the wrong family. They defend Lyric. Naturally.

"You have got to be joking. He was devoted to you." Ellery rolls her eyes. "It was kind of disgusting."

"Wrong response. You're supposed to support me, not Lyric."

"This information is surprising. Lyric was obviously in love with you and not showing any signs of boredom with the relationship."

"Thanks for the relationship evaluation, Nerd."

Lilac appears puzzled. "Am I supposed to be offended by the word nerd?"

"Can we get back to Lyric's supposed infidelity now?"

"Supposed?" I hiss at Ellery. "I saw them with my own two eyes."

"Start at the beginning," Juniper requests. "I was barely fourteen when you two broke it off. I don't remember what happened."

I study my sisters. They're all staring at me in eager anticipation. They can't wait to hear about my heartache. It's beginning to become painfully obvious why I couldn't escape town fast enough after college graduation.

I clear my throat. "It was after I left to move to Dallas. I made it about six hours before I turned around and came back. I went straight to Lyric's house, but he wasn't home. He was partying at the bar. The day I left. He was partying," I hiss.

"Continue," Lilac orders.

"I entered the bar and there he was, cozied up to Love Hill. They were making out in the back booth. I turned around, got back in my car, and drove all night until I arrived in Dallas."

"That did not happen," Ellery claims.

"I saw them!"

She shakes her head. "No, you saw Love Hill attack an off his face Lyric. He forced her off him and she fell to the floor. I remember because she was wearing this tiny skirt and when she fell, she mooned everyone. And it was a full moon since she wasn't wearing underwear." She shivers. "Phoenix and River dragged a very drunk Lyric home afterwards."

"You're one-hundred percent positive? You're not making this up?"

"Why would I make this up?"

"Maybe because you think if Lyric and I get back together, I'll stay in town."

"I know you will, but it doesn't mean I'm making this up." She pauses. "Think about it. Have you ever seen Love Hill and Lyric together?"

"I have it on good authority Love Hill showed up at the police station and asked Lyric out this week and he said no," Juniper adds.

"It would appear, big sis, that appearances can be deceiving. You should have fact-checked."

I hiss at Lilac and her logical brain.

But are my sisters right? Did Lyric not cheat on me? Have I been holding a grudge this entire time over something that never happened?

Chapter 12

Chipmunk – an animal that's supposed to burrow and not climb bookshelves

I flip the closed sign to open. It's time to re-open *Fall Into a Good Book*. Unfortunately, there's no grand opening party as Saffron wasn't lying about the state of her financial affairs. I'd be happy to pay for the party out of my personal funds, but the very idea of reviewing my financial affairs makes me break out into a cold sweat. Needless to say, I haven't had any news from the insurance company yet.

I planned to make a 'now open' sign, put out some balloons, and call it a day, but this town would never allow me to do such a thing. Rowan donated some brownies and cookies, Lennon provided some refreshments, and Clove, of *Clove's Coffee Corner* fame, showed up with these adorable shots of coffees.

It may not be a 'grand' opening, but brownies and cookies spell party to me. I made up trays with drinks and goodies for my sisters to hand out. Of course, none of them has actually shown up yet.

Ellery rushes in through the back door. "I'm here. I'm here. Sorry. I had a late check-out who thought I would want to hear his twenty-minute analysis of my rooms and my business. Clue in, dude. No one wants to listen to you rant about the low flow toilet and its inability to get rid of the 'evidence'. What did he do? Take the biggest shit in history?"

"I think you're obsessed with bodily functions. Every time I see you, you tell me some new story about shit. Literal shit."

"Please tell me today's conversation will be more highbrow than defecation," Lilac says as she enters the bookstore.

I shove a tray into her hands. "Hand these out to people."

She glances around the empty store. "What people?"

"If you build it, they will come." Ellery points to the front window where a few tourists are peeking into the store's windows.

I open the door and use the doorstop – aka a piece of pottery bearing no resemblance to a pot whatsoever – to prop it open. I usher the tourists in, and they make a beeline for Ellery.

Eden follows them in carrying a large plant holder with a tree in it. "Happy opening, Aspen."

Eden owns the florist shop, *Eden's Garden,* in town. Although, it doesn't resemble any other florist shop I've ever seen. She doesn't sell cut flowers. Between the waste from clippings and the rubber bands to tie the flowers together, it's not considered an environmentally sound business for Winter Falls. Instead, she sells trees and flowering plants.

"Thank you, Eden." I try to relieve her of the planter, but she refuses to let it go.

"I know exactly where it should be." Eden's also a devotee of feng shui.

"As you wish." She hurries away and I know I'll spend the evening putting things back to the way they were when I opened. Feng shui – or at least Eden's version of it – and retail display optimized for selling do not go together.

"Aspen!" Feather greets as she enters the store. "I brought you a gift."

I sigh when I open the paper bag from *Sensual Scents* to find a massage candle inside. Someone doesn't know when to quit. But I do know better than to say I don't need the candle. She'll have me set up on a date with the Chief of Police faster than I can pull the candle out of the bag.

"Thank you, Feather."

"Are you restarting the book club?"

"I am. Let me show you to the display with this month's book." I guide her to the book club display.

She frowns when she spots the book I've chosen. "*Klara and the Sun* by Kazuo Ishiguro." Her nose wrinkles in distaste. "This won't do. An intellectual book narrated by artificial intelligence. No, no, no."

"But I can't wait to read *Klara and the Sun*. I loved *Never Let Me Go*."

"Feel free to read it, but we won't be discussing it for book club."

I rub my temples where I feel a headache coming on. "Saffron told me I'd have full discretion with the store."

"The store? Yes. Boring book club picks? No."

She aims straight for the romance section while I chase after her. "This'll do." She waves a book with a half-naked man wearing a kilt on the cover.

"You didn't bother to read the blurb."

"Don't need to. If there's a sexy guy on the cover, it's a good book in my opinion."

"Tell the rest of the group we're reading," she checks the title, "*Fling With A Highlander.*"

"Okay," I give in. "But I want to try something different."

"As long as we're reading sexy novels, I'm good with whatever changes you make."

"I thought I'd provide wine and cheese and charge everyone ten dollars to attend."

I hold my breath and wait for her response. Charging attendees at book club was a good idea in the big city, but I'm worried how Winter Falls residents will respond.

"As long as you have some of the cheddar Phoenix makes, charge away," she says and marches off to the cash register where Ashlyn is waiting to check her out.

"I guess I better change the book club book display," I mutter as I grab several copies of *Fling With A Highlander*.

I'm finishing the display when Forest from the pet store *Unleashed* enters. He's holding onto a leash. He's not escorting a dog, though. No, Forest is out walking his chipmunk. Yes, chipmunk.

"Hey Forest. You may want to keep an eye on your chipmunk—"

Before I can finish telling him my dog is on the premises, Waffles barks and rushes toward the chipmunk who strains against his leash. Forest tightens his hold, but he's no match for a terrified animal. The tiny animal drags him forward.

I block Waffles, and he barges right into me. I lose my footing and fall back straight into Forest. We tumble to the floor, and the chipmunk breaks free.

"Chip!" Forest yells as he scrambles to his feet. "Get back here this instance."

Chip doesn't listen. He jumps onto the nearest bookshelf and scurries to the top. Waffles barks and scratches at the shelving. He can't climb, but he can cause the shelf to come tumbling to the ground. Not on my watch. I grab hold of his collar and yank, but my dog is not to be deterred.

I try another tactic. "How about a cookie, boy?"

By now everyone in the store has stopped browsing and is staring at my dog pawing at the bookshelves. As I watch, the bookshelves begin to totter. *No. No. No.* This can't be good. I glance up at the chipmunk to make sure he's safe and I swear he's staring down at my dog with a smirk on his face. This is the worst opening day ever.

"I got this." Juniper plows past me. "Here boy. Guess what I have."

Waffles stops barking long enough to sniff at the treat she's holding out to him. Juniper and her doggy treats to the rescue! She always has them in her pockets. And if she doesn't have pockets, she's been known to shove them down her bra.

"Come on." She holds out the treat while backing away from the shelf Chip is perched upon.

My dog trots after her until the two are shut behind the door to the backroom.

"Show's over, everyone. Please feel free to continue browsing the book selection. And, if you're interested in chipmunks such as Chip here, may I suggest our non-fiction animal section in the back?"

People trickle away until I'm alone with Forest. "What were thinking?"

"Chip gets lonely when I leave him behind. Since his brother Dale got adopted, he's been depressed."

"Please tell me my sister didn't adopt Dale."

He whistles and looks away. One of these days Juniper is going to go too far, and Ashlyn will end up killing her.

I motion to the shelf. "Can you get Chip down and take him away, please?"

Forest reaches up and captures Chip like he's a pet and not the wild animal he actually is. The man always did have a way with animals.

"I told you Winter Falls is more fun than going to Cancun on vacation," I hear someone whisper from behind a shelf. I inch closer to listen. It's not eavesdropping when it's my store.

"The people in this town are crazy. Is it even legal to own a ground squirrel?"

"It was a chipmunk, not a ground squirrel."

"What's the difference? Never mind. What does it matter? We should be on a beach somewhere drinking cocktails and hitting on foreigners."

"There's no need to find a foreigner to hit on. Have you seen the Chief of Police? Aye caramba."

And now I'm done eavesdropping. Not because I'm jealous. Lyric can date whoever he wants. He has been for the past ten years. What's to stop him now? Not me. My stomach cramps at the idea of seeing Lyric with another woman, but I tell it to knock it off. Lyric doesn't belong to me.

"Can I help you?"

"Yes. I'm searching for any books about the town of Winter Falls. Anything with local legends or about the history of the town."

"I'm sorry. We don't have any books about the town itself."

"Oh. Can you tell me where the local tourist office is?"

"There isn't a local tourist office." Her face falls. "Are you staying at *The Inn on Main*?" She nods. "Great. My sister owns it. She has a whole bunch of information about local attractions and tours you can do."

They scurry off, making sure to take another free brownie on their way. I can hardly blame them. Rowan bakes like a god.

"It's not a bad idea," Lilac says, and I nearly jump out of my skin.

"Don't sneak up on me."

"I didn't sneak. I walked over like a perfectly normal person."

I rub my chest where my heart is trying to fight its way out of my torso. "Whatever. What did you mean by it's not a bad idea?"

"There isn't a tourist office in town despite how much tourism we get. You could put some of the pamphlets for local attractions here."

"Not only pamphlets. I could carry some books about the region as well. Old Man Mercury wrote a book about Winter Falls, didn't he? Oh." I clap my hands as I warm to the idea. "You know what else would be a great addition? An area with local products available exclusively in town. Such as the local beer and cheese."

"You sound quite excited about a business idea when you have no plan to stay 'long-term'."

"You're using air quotes the wrong way," I tell her to hide my annoyance at her having a valid point. "I'm trying to help Saffron to develop a viable business. It would be a shame if Winter Falls didn't have a bookstore."

"I think this is one of those instances where I have to let you figure things out for yourself," she says before venturing off.

Figure things out for myself? What's there to figure out? I'm staying at my childhood home while I'm down on my luck until the insurance company cuts me the check I deserve. It's not rocket science.

Chapter 13

Misconception – a misunderstanding that can ruin ten years of your life Lyric

LYRIC

The bell over the door at *Fall Into a Good Book* rings when I enter. Aspen glances up and smiles my way, but once she realizes who it is, her smile drops from her face.

I lift the pot of lavender up. "Happy opening."

She comes around the desk, and I hand her the pot. She lifts it to her nose and inhales. "It smells lovely."

"I'm sorry I couldn't make it to the opening. One of Phoenix's goats from his diary farm got loose and decided to terrorize the animals at the sanctuary."

"Let me guess, my sister Juniper was suspiciously close to the farm when the 'escape' happened. I wouldn't be surprised if she thinks the goat is in love with one of the sanctuary animals and should be free to express his love."

I shrug. "Love is love. Apparently, even if it is between a goat and a bighorn sheep."

She snorts. "A goat would be crushed by a bighorn sheep." She studies the pot I brought the lavender in. "Is this one of Soleil's pots?"

"It is."

Her eyes widen. "Wow. She's getting better at throwing pots."

"Her business has taken off since she realized throwing pots doesn't mean literally throwing pots at the wall."

She giggles. "Remember when she threw the clay across the room in eleventh grade? I thought we'd be scrubbing the wall forever."

"I still don't understand why we had to help scrub the wall," I grump.

She rolls her eyes. "You? Scrub a wall? As I recall, you snuck off at the first opportunity."

I step closer and lower my voice. "And as I recall, you were right there with me." I have fond memories of the day we snuck off to the falls and went skinny dipping in the river.

She clears her throat and steps away from me. "I never claimed to be a pillar of the society unlike someone else, Mr. Chief of Police."

"Speaking of pillar of society, I'm sorry if I scared you the other night when I thought you were a burglar."

She sets the pot on the counter before answering. "It's fine. You couldn't have known Feather was setting you up."

"I think she was trying to set *us* up."

Aspen ignores my attempt to steer this conversation toward what she said the other night.

"At least she didn't give you a massage candle and tell you to have some fun."

I bark out a laugh. "Petal stopped by today, did she?"

"Between all the locals coming to 'support' the store, a chipmunk climbing the shelves, and my sister not knowing how to use the cash register, it's been a day."

Her words and obvious tiredness make me pause. I didn't merely come here to congratulate her on the opening. I also have questions about some things she said the other night. But those questions will have to wait.

"Have you eaten?" I have this need to feed her, although I doubt she'd appreciate any efforts on my part to take care of her.

"I did. Mom dropped by with a plate of meatloaf and mashed potatoes."

I groan. "Principal Ruby's meatloaf is the best."

"I have some left if you want it."

I hold up a hand to stop her. "I'm good." And how did my wanting to feed her and take care of her end up with her offering me food? This conversation is not going the way I expected it to.

"Are you nearly finished up here? Do you need me to walk you home?"

"Walk me home? This is Winter Falls, I'll be safe walking home."

"You never know." I waggle my eyebrows at her. "Juniper may let another goat free."

She points to her dog sleeping in the corner. "Waffles will save me."

The dog doesn't move upon hearing his name. "He appears to be a great guard dog."

"Just you wait. If any chipmunks attack, Waffles is on the job."

At the word chipmunk, the dog lifts his head.

"Chipmunks." I chuckle. "I heard what happened with Chip today."

The dog stands and howls.

"I am going to kill Forest," she grumbles before leaning over to calm her dog.

Her heart-shaped ass is on full display and my hands itch to reach forward to touch her. But I don't have the right to touch her the way I want to. I haven't had the right in a long time. Not since the day she drove away from town without looking back.

My hands fist. I might still love the woman, but I don't know if I can forgive her for deserting me. She said we'd keep in touch, but my phone calls and emails went unanswered. I thought she forgot all about me, but I'm beginning to think there's more to the story. A story I'm determined to get to the bottom of. But when Aspen yawns, I realize I won't be getting any answers tonight.

"If you don't need anything, I'll be on my way."

She rolls her eyes. "Say what you came here to say first."

I scratch at the growth of my beard. "How do you know I wasn't just checking in?"

She snorts. "Please. I know you better than that. You came strutting in here like you were on a mission. What do you want?"

"Can we sit down?" I motion to the set of armchairs in the corner of the store.

"Oh boy. This is a sit down conversation. Should I contact my lawyer?"

"Stop being a smart ass and sit your butt down."

"Yes, sir. Whatever you say, sir."

My cock stirs at her sassiness. I always did love her sass. It got us in tons of trouble while we were in school, but I wouldn't change all those hours of detention for the world.

I wait until we've settled in the chairs to speak. "You've said a few confusing things since you came home," I start.

"And now I'm confused," she sasses right back at me.

"I'm being serious here."

"Sorry. Proceed." She toes off her sandals and sits cross-legged in the chair.

Here goes nothing. "You called me a cheater and said Love Hill stole me away. I have to admit I'm awfully confused about those remarks since I'm not a cheater and I never had any sort of relationship with Love Hill."

Her green eyes spark with anger and she crosses her arms over her chest. "Really? We're outright lying to each other now?"

"I'm not lying. I swear on my badge I have no idea what you're talking about."

She uncrosses her legs and jumps to her feet. "You're unbelievable. It's been a decade and still you won't come clean. All these years of waiting for you to apologize. You're never going to apologize. It's a good thing I'm not staying here long."

Not staying long? I assumed with all the changes she's making at the bookstore that she'd decided to stay in Winter Falls longer. Once again, I'm wrong about her. My heart burns, but I ignore it. Now isn't the time to worry about the future. The past is the current topic of discussion.

I stand and hold up my hands to try to calm her down. "I can't apologize for something I didn't do."

She pokes me in the chest. "I saw you," she seethes. "I saw you kissing Love Hill."

I rear back. "When? My lips have never touched hers."

She throws her hands in the air. "And the lies continue. After all this time."

I take a deep breath before I lose my temper. When one isn't enough, I take another one. Aspen West drives me crazy on the best of days. But now she's lost her dang mind.

I grasp her hands and draw her flush to me. "I am not lying. Maybe if you explain what you think you saw, I can figure out what really happened."

Her eyes narrow and she tries to tug her hands away, but I hold tight. I'm not letting go until I figure out what the hell she's talking about.

"Fine. I'll tell you. But after this, I'm done with you. No lavender pots. No reminiscing about sneaking out to the falls during school time to go swimming. Nothing. Do you understand?"

I nod. "I understand." Notice I didn't say I agree to her terms.

"I came back," she begins and my heart stops. She came back? When?

"I made it about six hours out of town before I couldn't go any further." She swallows. "Like a lovesick fool, I turned the car around and drove six hours straight back here. When I finally found you, you were at *Electric Vibes*. You were in a corner booth with Love all over you. I went to yell at you, but your lips locked with Love's, and I was done. I marched my ass right out of there, got into my car, and drove until I couldn't stay awake any longer."

A tear escapes and rolls down her cheek. I wipe it away with my thumb.

"I don't remember the night you left."

Her nostrils flare. "Yeah, because you went out and partied."

I wrap my arms around her and draw her body flush to mine. "I did go out. But I wasn't partying. It's called drowning your sorrows. I'm ashamed to say it, but I don't remember kissing Love. I am sorry you had to witness us together, though. If I had known you came back…"

I pause because I don't want to admit the next part.

"If you had known …. What?"

"I would have jumped in your car and gone to Dallas with you."

She leans back to look me in the eyes. "You would have left Winter Falls for me?" I nod. "But you said you'd never leave."

"That was before you drove away."

"And you didn't get together with Love Hill?"

"Sunshine, I have never wanted Love. My brothers dragged me out of the bar that night and I had a hangover for two days."

The bell over the door rings and I glance over my shoulder to find Ellery standing in the doorway. Her eyes widen as her lips tip up. "Oops! Sorry. I didn't know you were busy. I'll catch you later, Aspen."

At Ellery's words, the spell is broken and Aspen shuffles away from me.

"Thank you for telling me the truth. I need to get back to work now."

I let her retreat. I just cleared up a misconception she's had for a decade. I can give her time to think about it.

"Have a good night, Sunshine." I lean over and kiss her cheek before strolling out of the store.

I whistle as I stroll toward the police station. The anger I've been carrying around for the past decade about the love of my life deserting me dissipates as I go. Poor Aspen thought I cheated on her. She must have been heartbroken. No wonder she never returned my calls or emails.

I wish she'd said something before this instead of letting all these years pass by, but I can hardly blame her. She thought I ran straight into another woman's arms after she left. As if I would ever cheat on my girl. And make no mistake about it, she is *my* girl.

Chapter 14

Jealousy — an emotion with no basis in reality whatsoever

"I told you Lyric didn't cheat," Ellery sings.

"Don't gloat," I tell her. "It's unattractive."

"I'm feeling pretty attractive right now." She whirls around with her arms out and her skirt flies up around her.

"There is a fair bit of evidence to suggest a person's attractiveness is affected by their personality," Lilac, our walking talking *Scientific American*, chimes in.

"Leave the nerd at the door," Juniper says as she motions toward the bar.

"I thought we were on an after-dinner stroll. No one said anything about going out."

I look down at my clothes. I'm wearing an old Colorado State University t-shirt with a stain on the boob and a pair of jean shorts I cut off myself and didn't exactly do the best job at. There's a reason I left these clothes behind when I left.

"You're fine." Ellery grabs my arm and drags me toward the door.

I plant my feet and we come to a screeching halt. "I look like something the cat dragged in."

"Don't be ridiculous. You're entirely too large for a cat to drag in. Unless you're referring to a mountain cat aka a cougar. A male cougar can reach up to two-hundred pounds. But you wouldn't want one to drag you anywhere."

Ashlyn slaps Lilac. "You're not helping."

"I fail to understand why correcting a person's misconceptions isn't helping."

"Don't worry. Lyric will think you're hot no matter what you wear." Ashlyn waggles her eyebrows.

"I wonder if Rowan will be at the bar," I say and enjoy the show as her cheeks turn the color of fire hydrants.

My little sister is no wallflower, though. As I watch, she straightens her back.

"I guess we'll have to go inside to find out."

And, because I was too busy paying attention to Ashlyn and not enough to my other sisters, Ellery and Juniper manage to push me inside the bar. The door bangs shut behind us and everyone watches as we enter.

"Hide the good stuff. The West sisters have arrived," Lennon hollers with a huge grin on his face.

"I resemble that remark," I say before using the bar to propel me high enough to kiss his cheek.

"You girls need a pitcher of margaritas?"

"Not tonight. I'm working tomorrow. I'll have an IPA. I heard the new *Naked Falls* IPA is good."

Lennon sets the beer on the counter before leaning over and placing his elbows on the bar as if he's settling in for a chat. "How's it going at the bookstore?"

"Okay, I guess. It's only the first week."

"Things haven't been going the best for the store and Saffron."

"How did I not know Saffron was suffering?"

He shrugs. "Maybe you should come around for more than a few days over the holidays." And, with his parting shot lodged in its target, he knocks on the bar before moving away. "Have a good one."

I grab my beer and follow my sisters to a booth. It's early yet and the place is relatively quiet.

Ellery elbows me. "Lyric's here." She points to where he's sitting with his brothers in another booth. When he notices me, I wave my beer at him.

"Mom and Dad aren't here now. I want to hear the whole story of how you found out Lyric didn't cheat," she demands. "Something, may I remind you, we already told you about."

I sip on my beer to buy myself some time. "There isn't much to tell," I finally say. "We talked. Cleared the air. End of story."

"Boring story," Lilac says, and everyone glares at her. "What? It was. A story should always incorporate drama. Her story had zero drama."

"No worries." Ashlyn sits back in her seat. "The drama has apparently come to us."

"What are you talking about?"

She points with her beer bottle at Lyric's table where the two women I overheard talking at the bookstore the other day are joining them.

"Someone has a date," Juniper chants.

I shrug. "Good for him."

My stomach cramps, but I ignore it. Lyric is free to be with whoever he wants to. I don't own him. I face away from their table. I don't need to witness him with a date.

"It's Barbie and Stacie with ie not y."

Lilac frowns at Ellery. "You're serious. Their names are based upon a toy?"

"They're staying at the inn."

I can't help myself and glance over to observe one of them – I don't know and don't care if it's Barbie or Stacie – leaning over the table. Her skirt lifts and I get a glimpse of her butt cheek. The last thing I need is to see her perfect ass. I divert my gaze.

"At least you won't have to worry about digging granny panties out of the toilet with those girls."

Five new beers are slammed down on the table. "Don't worry about those girls, Aspen. An out-of-towner can never hold our Lyric's attention," Lennon says before wandering off.

"Although, he did date ..." Ashlyn screws up her eyes before snapping her fingers "... Katie for at least a year."

"Katie? Who's Katie? Why haven't I heard of her before?" And why do I sound like a jealous cow? "Never mind. None of my business." I reach for a bottle of beer.

"Even I can tell you're lying," Lilac says, and I stick my tongue out at her.

"I'm going to the ladies' room."

Ellery grabs my hand before I can leave. "Do you need me to come with you?"

I wrest my hand out of her hold. "I got this. I've been able to pee by myself for thirty years now. I'm actually quite proud of myself in this regard."

"Why would you—" Lilac's question dies on her lips. "Let me guess, this is sarcasm."

I point at her. "You got it!"

I march off toward the hallway. I keep my focus firmly on the floor in front of me while reminding myself how I don't care what Lyric's doing.

It was hard enough convincing myself those words were true when I thought he was a cheater. Now I know he didn't cheat on me with Love Hill, it's way more difficult. I'm not here long term, I remind myself.

After I take care of my business, I study myself in the mirror. I'm a mess. My sisters could have warned me we were coming to the bar and given me a chance to at least put a bit of lip gloss on. Instead, I'm completely make-upless and the curls in my hair are out of control. I try using a bit of water to tame my curls, but it's a lost cause.

I exit the bathroom and turn toward the bar, but someone grabs my arm and yanks me in the other direction. I don't scream because I recognize the hand. There's a scar on the webbing between his thumb and forefinger from where River poked him with a stick. You never, ever get between an Alston and a s'more.

I allow Lyric to haul me down the hallway and out the backdoor. As soon as we're outside, though, I wrest my arm out of his hold.

"What are you doing?" I hiss at him.

"I wanted to explain."

"Explain? Explain about what?"

Oh no, are there more revelations to be made? I usually limit my life-altering revelations to one per month. Life-altering? Nope. Finding out Lyric's not a cheater is not life-altering. It's not. I'm not staying in Winter Falls forever, remember?

"I'm not out on a date."

He's not? "Yeah, sure. Whatever."

He steps closer, and I retreat until my back hits the wall.

"I saw the tourist earlier today and she asked where the best place to have a drink is. I told her here, but I didn't ask her to join me."

I roll my eyes. "She was obviously coming on to you when she asked where the best place to have a drink is."

He shrugs and because he's got me backed into the wall, I feel his muscles bunch. I remember how those muscles felt ten years ago. Based on how his shirt now strains to contain them, they've obviously gotten harder and more defined since then.

"Lots of tourists ask me about where to do things in town. Being Chief of Police in Winter Falls is half keeping the town safe and half dealing with the tourists," he says and draws my attention away from his body.

Good thing, too. My hand was already lifting to touch. Bad hand! Time to change the topic of conversation.

"This is why I'm thinking a corner of the bookstore should be devoted to tourist things since we don't have a local tourist office. I could put maps of the town as well as pamphlets out. Maybe add a display of local products."

"Great idea, Sunshine."

My heart skips a beat at his use of my former nickname. When Lyric realized how much I hate my middle name Cloud, he started calling me Sunshine. *Don't get used to it, Aspen. Don't fall into his trap.*

"In fact, you should come to the next town meeting and present your idea. I bet you could get some type of stipend for acting as the tourist office."

"You mean Saffron could get a stipend," I say to remind myself as much as him about my temporary status. "And she should be the one to present the idea since it's her store."

He shrugs and steps back. "Saffron won't mind if you present the idea. It is your idea after all."

I know Saffron wouldn't mind. Every time I've phoned her to discuss an idea with her, she hasn't bothered to listen before telling me to 'run with it'. I'm getting worried about her. She used to love the bookstore, but now it seems she's lost all interest.

Lyric tags my hand and leads me toward the back entrance. "We better get back in before the town has us married off."

I try to tug my hand away, but he holds strong. "If you don't let go of my hand, there will definitely be rumors."

He glances back over his shoulder at me and winks. "Let them talk."

I narrow my eyes on him. What is he up to? Before I have a chance to ask, he deposits me with my sisters, kisses my cheek, tells me to have a nice night, and saunters off. What just happened?

Chapter 15

A list – a device used to embarrass your children

"Aspen! Get down here, now!"

Geez. There's nothing like your mother yelling at you to get out of your room to make your thirty-three-year-old self feel like a teenager. If I were a teenager, I'd stomp my foot and ignore her. But I'm an adult, which means I stick to ignoring her and don't bother stomping my foot.

"Yeah, Aspen. Stop mooning over Lyric and get down here," Ellery hollers.

Ellery's here, too? It must be time for Sunday dinner. Which means all of my sisters are here. Great. They'll yell taunts up the stairs until I'm forced out of my room to deal with them. So much for hiding.

"I'm not mooning over Lyric," I claim when I enter the living room where my sisters have gathered for our weekly Sunday dinner.

"After what happened on Friday night, she's probably reminiscing instead of mooning," Ashlyn – the little shit stirrer – says.

"What happened on Friday night? Did Lyric and Aspen finally reacquaint themselves with each other in a sexual manner?"

I bury my face in my hands and groan. Why can't I have parents who pretend sex doesn't happen? I know those parents exist. I went to college. I made friends. None of their parents talked about sex at the dinner table when I visited.

Needless to say, those friends thought it was 'totally cool' my parents were open about sex. Easy to say when it's not your mom and dad debating the pros and cons of lubricated versus textured condoms at Sunday dinner.

"He dragged her out of the bar into the backyard," Juniper tattles.

"Don't you have your own lives? Ones that don't involve giving your big sister a hard time? What do you do when I'm not around?"

My mom shackles my wrist and drags me toward the kitchen.

"We make fun of Ashlyn and Rowan," Ellery yells after us.

"Ignore them," Mom orders me.

I point over my shoulder to where my sisters followed us. "Hard to ignore them. They're like a pack of street dogs. They follow me everywhere."

Ashlyn wrinkles her nose. "If we're going to be compared to dogs, can we at least be pure breeds?"

"Pure breeds!" Juniper shrieks. "Do you know what they do to those poor animals at puppy farms? Breeding dogs is an abomination and should be illegal."

"Besides, pure breed animals are much weaker than mixed breeds," Lilac points out.

Waffles barks before racing into the kitchen to join us. I guess my beagle/shepherd mix agrees with my sister Lilac. Before I can kneel down to pet my baby boy, Juniper is already feeding him treats, and – slut that he is – he rolls onto his back to expose his belly for her to rub.

"I thought we were in here to discuss Aspen's sexy times with Lyric outside of Dad's hearing range," Ellery says, and I snap my teeth at her. She couldn't let the topic change to the pros and cons of breeding dogs?

"Don't worry, girls. Your dad's hearing is perfectly fine. In fact, every function on the man is in working order." Mom waggles her eyebrows, and I gag.

"Stop! I don't want to hear about how my parents have sex."

"I don't know why not. It's perfectly natural."

"No, Mom. It's not perfectly natural to talk about your sex life with your parents."

She frowns at me. "It should be. Perhaps I'll add the topic to our sexual education curriculum."

Ashlyn groans. "Anyone else feel sorry for the students at the high school?"

"The high school?" Mom tsks. "Sex education should begin much earlier. I prefer elementary school, but the board continues to insist on middle school."

While Mom begins her tried and true tirade on teaching sex-ed in school, I decide now is the perfect time to sneak away.

I inch toward the sliding glass door to the backyard. I have my hand on the handle when Ellery yells, "Aha! I caught you."

I ignore her and slide the door open before running outside. Waffles bounds out the door after me. He flies off the deck and hits my legs with such force we end up in a heap on the grass. He licks at my face, and I push him away.

"Your breath is gross," I say while keeping his snout as far away from my face as possible.

"You need to brush his teeth," Juniper admonishes.

"Are you done rolling in the grass now?" Dad asks. "I'm hungry and there's a documentary on recovering wildlife after the fires in Australia on soon."

"I want to watch that, too," Juniper says as she follows Dad inside.

I get to my feet and brush the grass off my shorts. "You are trouble, baby boy. Trouble."

He woofs and gives me a doggy smile, not at all concerned with my reprimand. Darn it. He's too cute to stay mad at.

Once everyone is seated around the table, Mom lifts the lid on the dish in the middle of the table with a flourish. "Ta da!"

We lean forward to peer into the pot. "What is it?"

"Sweet corn risotto with roasted shallots."

It doesn't sound bad. If you grow up in Winter Falls, you learn to appreciate all kinds of food. When every meal you eat consists of locally grown, seasonal products, you learn to be creative with food. Ask me how many types of potato soups there are sometime.

"Are you on a vegan kick again?" Juniper asks as she scoops food onto her plate and everyone at the table groans.

The last time Mom went on a vegan kick, I was in high school. Take my word for it. Adding a substantial amount of legumes to a family's diet is not a good idea when you only have two bathrooms in your house. Seriously. Don't try this at home.

"Nope. I saw the recipe on the town Facebook page and decided to give it a try."

"Have you heard from the insurance company yet?" Dad asks, and I frown.

"Yeah, I got an email on Friday. It's as you expected. They offered me a settlement."

"Those damn insurance companies. Always trying to make a buck off the sweat of the working class."

"Dad, we're hardly working class," I point out.

"I work, don't I? Your mother works, doesn't she? And you worked your heinie off getting your bookstore to turn a profit. How come we're not working class?"

Lilac doesn't hesitate to answer him. "The working class refers to the social group of people who are primarily employed in unskilled or semi-skilled manual or industrial work. A lawyer and school principal hardly work manual labor."

"Plus," Juniper points her fork at him, "your father owns a bunch of grocery stores."

"Which he worked very hard at."

Mom sighs. "You are the most bull-headed man I know."

"Because I'm right."

"Bull-headed," she murmurs under her breath.

"Personally, I want to hear what the company offered Aspen," Lilac says, and all eyes focus on me.

"Slightly over half what I should be getting."

"Slightly over half!" Dad pounds his fist on the table. "I have a mind to go down to Dallas and tell those yahoos what I think of them."

"Aren't all insurance companies headquartered in Omaha, Nebraska? I thought I saw a documentary about it once." Ashlyn says in her Little Miss Innocent voice. Innocent? Hardly.

"Even better. Omaha is closer. Who's up for a road trip?"

I lean close to Ellery and whisper, "Did he forget he doesn't own a car?"

She rolls her eyes. "He always forgets he doesn't own a car."

"I don't think it was a documentary," Lilac says. "I believe you're referring to the movie *Up In the Air* and I don't think the main character played by George Clooney worked for an insurance company."

"Don't you love George Clooney? He's on my list," Mom says.

I groan. Here we go again.

"Your list?" Ashlyn gulps. "You have a list of men you're allowed to have sex with who aren't Dad?"

"Of course, I do. Doesn't everyone have a list?"

Dad raises his hand. "I have one."

"Who's on it?"

My mouth drops open at Lilac's question. "What is wrong with you? Do you seriously want to know who's on Dad's list?"

"You know how much I enjoy sociology, although referring to sociology as a science is quite far-fetched. Science involves testing that can be repeated where the outcome will always be the same. Patterns do not make science."

Dad ignores her dig on sociology and answers her original question. "Cate Blanchett, Nicole Kidman, Jennifer Lopez, Robin Wright. Oh, and Viola Davis. Her performance in *Fences*? Marvelous. Simply marvelous."

"There's a reason she won the Oscar for her performance," Juniper agrees.

"Who's on your list, Mom?" Lilac asks, and I kick her under the table. "Ow. Are you having muscle spasms? You should drink more water. It will help."

Mom counts them off on her fingers. "I already said George Clooney. Who else? There's Brad Pitt, Pierce Brosnan, Barack Obama, Colin Firth, Jimmy Smits, Jon Bon Jovi, and Jennifer Lopez."

"Jennifer Lopez?"

Mom shrugs. "What? I'm bi-curious."

Dad winks at her. "I thought you satisfied your bi-curiosity in college."

She waggles her eyebrows at him. "But we never did try a threesome."

"And I'm out."

I stand and carry my plate to the kitchen wondering if Ellery will let me stay in one of her vacant rooms at the inn for the remainder of my stay in Winter Falls.

Chapter 16

Railroad – not only a set of tracks upon which trains run

"I don't know why I'm here. I don't own a business in town," I grumble as we enter the town hall for the monthly town business meeting.

"I don't own a business and I'm here," Juniper says.

"This is the best entertainment all month in Winter Falls," Ashlyn adds. "Popcorn?" She waves a bag at me.

"Where did you get popcorn?"

She points to the rear of the room where there's a concession stand set up.

"They sell food and drinks at a town meeting?"

Ellery laces her arm through mine and drags me to the front row. "Hurry up. I don't want to miss out on the best seats."

"I don't remember the town meeting being this big of an attraction when we were growing up."

"There's a strict age limit."

I giggle – an age limit in a town where nudity is encouraged? – but stop when I notice she's completely serious. "You're serious?"

Ashlyn leans over Ellery to answer. "It's strictly enforced, too. I tried coming to the meeting two days before my twenty-first birthday and was thrown out."

"Thrown out?" Juniper rolls her eyes. "As I recall you ended up on a date with Peace."

"Usually I find the names of the people in this town a bit odd, but I sincerely enjoy the congruity of a police officer having Peace as a first name," Lilac comments.

"Here." Ashlyn thrusts a beer into my hand before passing out bottles to the rest of my sisters.

"I didn't ask for a beer."

"Each time someone says the word 'but', you have to drink."

"But—"

"Drink!" Ashlyn shouts and my sisters – including Lilac – lift their beers and drink.

"This is ridiculous. We're going to get smashed considering how many times b—... *that* word is used in normal conversation."

"Shush," Ashlyn hisses. "It's starting."

Forest ambles to the table set up in front of the room. In addition to owning the local pet store, *Unleashed,* he's the mayor. The town business owners take turns being mayor as having mayoral elections is 'unfair', 'undemocratic', and 'a personality contest'.

He hits a gavel against the table. "Hear ye, hear ye. I hereby call this town hall meeting of Winter Falls to order."

He waits while everyone quiets down and finds their seat. "We have several agenda items this evening, but—"

Ellery elbows me and nods to my beer. I sigh – such a silly game – but I do take a sip.

"Our first item on the agenda is the Lammas Festival. Lilac, you have the floor."

Lilac stands and walks to the front of the room.

"Was Lilac in charge of the Lammas festival?" I whisper my question to Ellery.

"She's the comptroller of Winter Falls."

"Since when?" And why did no one tell me?

"Since Feather got high and used the town accounts to buy everyone in town an ice cream cone."

"Yeah," Ashlyn adds, "we thought she was doing a good deed since we were having a heatwave in April."

"But…" Juniper pauses, and we all drink from our beers, "then she showed up to the next town meeting and requested a permit to expand *Feather's Frozen Delights*."

"Ms. Fuddy Duddy aka our middle sister who is often confused with an android asked her where she would procure the funds for the expansion," Ellery says.

"And then," Ashlyn's whisper-shouting by now, "Feather said she had a windfall in April. She had zero recollection of buying everyone ice cream."

"Ahem!" Lilac clears her throat. "Perhaps my sisters could pay attention to the accounts instead of gossiping."

I feel my face heat. "Whatever you say, Lilac Bean."

Lilac purses her lips. She hates when anyone calls her Lilac Bean. And, like the good big sis I am, I make sure to use her middle name whenever I can for maximum effect.

"As I was saying …"

Fifteen minutes later – Fine! It was five, but it felt *way* longer – Lilac finally wraps up.

"I thought you said these things were good entertainment," I complain to Ashlyn.

She winks. "Wait for it."

Forest stands. "Thank you, Lilac, for your very thorough account of our financial standings after the Lammas Festival."

Lilac nods before returning to her seat. I hand her her beer. "You're behind."

"And now we have a request from Lennon, the owner of the *Electric Vibes* bar."

Lennon makes his way to the front of the room. He scratches his beard and hikes up his jeans before beginning.

"I'm here to petition the town to allow me to sell absinthe at the bar."

"But isn't absinthe illegal?" someone interrupts to ask.

"Drink!" Juniper and Ashlyn shout in unison.

"But it has medicinal properties."

"Drink!" Do Juniper and Ashlyn practice shouting in unison?

Forest slams his gavel against the table. "Quiet! Quiet!"

"But," Lennon complains.

"Drink!" Ashlyn yells.

Forest points to her. "You, too, Ashlyn Dream West."

Ashlyn mimics zipping her lips.

"Please continue Lennon."

"Well, I, uh …"

Ellery elbows me and points to Lyric who's strolling to the front of the room. "Doesn't he appear mighty fine in his uniform?"

"Mighty fine," mimics Ashlyn.

"Meh." I shrug. "He's wearing jeans and a uniform top. Not much of a uniform if you ask me."

My words are all lies. Lies, I tell you. Lyric is a wet dream come to life. His jeans are molded to his legs. Those strong thighs get me each and every time. While his uniform top strains to contain his wide shoulders, and his utility belt draws my attention to his narrow waist. A waist I've wrapped my arms around too many times to count.

Ashlyn shoves another beer in my hands. "You look like you could use a cold one."

Lyric's sky-blue eyes catch mine and he winks. My heart flutters and my stomach tingles. I drink before I decide to drag him out of here and have my wicked way with him.

Whoa. I need to slow down the drinking if I'm considering Lyric and I having sexy times together. Those days are gone, remember? My body warms. Nope. It doesn't remember.

"Chief Alston, you have the floor."

"I may not personally have a problem with Lennon serving absinthe but," he pauses and looks straight at me. When I don't drink, he nods to my beer. Oh, right. I drink and he continues, "I'm afraid absinthe is illegal."

Several townspeople jump to their feet, and he raises his hands for quiet.

"I'm afraid there's nothing we can do about this. U.S. Customs prohibits the import of absinthe."

"Damn government trying to rob me of all my rights," Lennon mutters.

"Or, the government is trying to protect citizens from having seizures."

Everyone starts talking all at once about whether the federal government – aka 'the man' – is trying to ruin our lives and strip us of all our freedoms. This discussion will go on all night if someone lets it. And, it wouldn't be the first time. Hippies do love to debate 'the man'.

Forest beats the gavel against the table until there's a modicum of quiet in the room. "Let's vote on it."

Lyric crosses his arms over his chest and plants his feet shoulder-width apart. "We will not vote on it. According to the town regulations, no ordinance shall be passed if it is against federal law."

"Yes, but—

I try sipping on my beer, but Ellery grabs hold of the bottle and tilts it upwards until I'm forced to shotgun the beer, drown, or wrestle the bottle out of her hands. I choose to shotgun the beer. Drowning is not on my agenda for the night and, let's face it, the chance of me wresting a bottle from her is non-existent. The woman's hands are freakishly strong.

Lyric slams his hands down on the table in front of the mayor and growls. "No buts. On this rule, I will not budge." He stands and addresses the rest of the crowd. "Hold all the sit-ins you want. This law is for public health and safety."

Juniper slaps a beer into my chest. "You're behind."

"Where is all this beer coming from?"

She points to an ice-filled bucket at Ashlyn's feet.

"They should raise the age for attendance of these things to twenty-five," I mutter, and Ashlyn sticks her tongue out at me.

"I'll agree to this," Mayor Forest says, "provided you and Aspen Cloud work together on the Mabon Festival Parade."

I rush to my feet. Bad idea. I feel woozy and unsteady on my feet. I grab hold of Ellery's shoulder to stop myself from crashing to the floor.

"The Mabon Festival Parade isn't for another month. I don't know if I'll be in town in a month."

"If you decide to run away again before the festival begins, you can hand your duties over to your sister." Forest waves in the general direction of my sisters who all mutter 'not it' under their breath.

"Run away? Leaving this town is not running away."

Lyric ignores my protest. "And don't forget her idea to add a town tourist center to the bookstore. We should vote on it."

"Wait!" I wail. "We can't vote on it. It's not my bookstore. Besides, it was only an idea."

"A sound idea," Forest declares. "All in favor of Aspen adding a tourist center to *Fall Into a Good Book*?"

"Aye!" is cried by several people in the room, including my traitor sisters. I glare at them, and they respond by batting their eyelashes like they're innocent. Innocent? Not hardly.

"The ayes have it." He pounds his gavel. "The motion carries."

"You didn't even ask for nays!"

Lilac sighs before getting to her feet. "I have to agree with Aspen Cloud on this one. We do need to ask if anyone opposes the motion."

"But—"

I barely get the word out before Juniper is tapping my beer and telling me to, "Drink!"

I drink because I know she'll continue to interrupt me until I do as she says.

"Anyone opposed to the motion?" Forest asks, and I scan the room. No one will meet my gaze.

He pounds his gavel again. "Motion carries." He smiles at me. "It's good you're integrating into the community. Helping with the Mabon Festival Parade and now opening a tourist center. Good for you, Aspen."

I throw my arms in the air before collapsing in my seat.

"Meeting adjourned."

"Come on," Ellery nudges me. "Everyone has a beer at the bar after the meeting."

"I'm good," I pout.

"Don't be such a baby. You didn't get what you wanted. You'll survive."

"Didn't get what I want? This is crazy. I didn't move back to town."

She cocks an eyebrow. "You didn't?"

"Never mind. Talking to anyone in this town is the equivalent of talking to a brick wall. Let's go get a drink."

Chapter 17

Trouble – difficulty or problems, not always unwelcome

I SURVEY THE CORNER of the bookshop I've done my best to turn into a cozy meeting place for the book club. The chairs are set up in a circle with a low table in the middle laden with wine and various cheeses. All from Phoenix's dairy farm, naturally. Lyric's brother Phoenix knows what he's doing when it comes to cheese, which is surprising since Phoenix thought school was merely a suggestion when we were kids.

"How many people are you expecting?" Ellery asks.

"Besides you four?" I shrug. "I don't know."

I may have coerced my sisters into attending the book club to ensure someone showed up tonight. After the town meeting, they owed me.

"I'm happy to attend a book club, but I don't understand why we read *Flight With A Highlander*," Lilac complains.

"Do you need me to explain the sex stuff to you?" Ashlyn asks.

"How do you know about the sex stuff?"

She rolls her eyes at me. "One, Mom gave me the sex talk when I was six. And, two, I went to college. I'm not a virgin."

"I thought you were saving all your loving for Rowan."

She raises an eyebrow. "You want to go there? You of 'I'm not running away' fame?"

The bell over the door rings before I can answer her and Feather, Petal, Sage, Cayenne, Clove, and Soleil stroll inside. I'm not surprised to see Feather. She did pick the book after all. But I didn't realize the other women were book lovers.

I greet everyone at the door and motion them toward the sitting area. Once we're settled, I pick up a copy of the book and begin.

"Shall we start with everyone saying whether they enjoyed the book or not?"

Ellery raises her hand. "I'll go. I loved it. It's a good replacement for my BOB, if you get what I mean." She waggles her brows.

"Who's Bob?" Feather asks. "Do you have an out-of-town lover?"

"Is it one of those friends with benefits arrangements?" Clove asks. "I always did want to try one of those."

"You've been married to the same man for thirty years," Feather points out.

"Thus, the reason I want to try a friend with benefits."

"There's no way Ellery has an out-of-town lover I don't know about," Sage declares.

Ellery smirks. "Maybe you don't know everything."

Lilac sighs. "Bob is not a person. It's her battery-operated boyfriend. Even I know that."

"Told you she didn't have a lover," Sage gloats.

I clap my hands. "If we could return to the discussion of the book now, please."

Feather leans over and whisper-shouts to Cayenne. "I told you Aspen would be strict."

"You didn't need to tell me. Have you seen her downward dog? The woman is uptight."

"Bet you're glad Mom had a teacher conference tonight, huh?" Ellery asks in a whisper.

I read the first chapter of the book and decided I wouldn't be inviting Mom. She would have fit right in with the other attendees, but I have no desire to discuss sex with my mother. Any more than she forces me to, at least.

"I have a question." Petal raises her hand, and I nod for her to go ahead. "How did they manage the sex position in Chapter 3? Me and Orion tried it and it damn near caused his back to go out."

"I wondered why he was walking funny yesterday."

"I believe you're referring to the butterfly position," Lilac says, and everyone gasps. "What? I'm twenty-nine and have a perfectly healthy sex life."

"You do?" Juniper asks before I get the chance.

"I'm confused. Why are you surprised?"

"Because she reminds me of a robot most of the time," Ellery mumbles to me, and I slap her.

"But who do you have sex with?" Juniper's not letting this go.

"Men. I'm heterosexual. I thought you knew this. Didn't Mom give you the 'it's okay to be who you are' speech?"

"We don't care whether you have sex with men or women!" Ashlyn shouts while throwing her hands in the air. I grab her glass of wine before she spills it. "We want details of who they are!"

"Oh. I have arrangements with several men."

"Arrangements?" Juniper snickers. "How sexy."

I clap my hands again. "The book, ladies. Can we talk about the book?"

Petal raises her hand again. "I have another question."

"Of course, you do," I mumble before raising my voice. "Is it about the book?" She smiles. "Go ahead."

"How many times can a man have sex in one night?"

"How is your question related to the book?"

I'm exasperated. This is not how a book club is supposed to go. We're supposed to be having an intellectual discussion about literature, not discussing sex.

"Define sex," Lilac asks.

"I thought you knew all about 'sex'." In case we don't catch Juniper's sarcasm, she uses air quotes around the word sex.

"Thence, my question. Sex has many aspects. There's cunnilingus, fellatio, anilingus, digital penetration, penal penetration... The list goes on and on. Not every incident requires a man's penis to recover."

I bury my hands in my face. I can't believe this is happening. Have I entered an alternate universe?

"Maybe we should have Lilac give us a lecture on the different aspects," Clove suggests, and I groan.

"I was referring to penal penetration," Petal answers in response to Lilac's question.

"I'm afraid I can't give you a scientific answer other than it depends on various factors."

"Maybe it's an age thing. Let's ask Aspen," Petal suggests.

I drop my hands from my face. "What? Why are we asking Aspen? I'm not the sex guru."

"What a good idea! We should find a sex guru to come talk to our next book club meeting." Clove claps.

"I thought Lilac was doing a sex lecture."

"Shush, Feather. I want to hear Aspen's answer."

Can I feign misunderstanding? I can try. "My answer about what?"

"How many times can Lyric do it in one night?"

I eye the exit. Surely, I can make it to the door before anyone catches me. I'm thirty years younger than most of the women in the group. They'll never catch me.

"Yeah, Asp. How many times can Lyric do it in one night?" Ellery smirks, and I decide sisters are overrated. From here on out, I'm an only child.

Since my eyes are focused on the door, I notice Lyric wander by. He catches my eye and smiles and waves. I shake my head at him, and mouth *run for your life.*

He obviously doesn't read lips as he opens the door and swaggers in with a smile plastered on his face.

"Did someone report a disturbance?"

Feather, Petal, and Sage scream. "A stripper? Aspen, you're our favorite bookstore owner ever."

"Are you high?" Not a good question to ask in Winter Falls. "Never mind. He's not a stripper. He's the Chief of Police."

"Why can't he be both?" Feather winks at Lyric, and his face darkens to the color of a sun ripened tomato.

I shrug. "I guess he could. What do you say, Chief? You want to strip for us?"

He rallies. Of course, he rallies. So much for witnessing Lyric run away with his tail tucked between his legs. The pictures would have been awesome.

"I'm sorry, ladies, but I'm afraid I'm a one woman man."

"Oh, come on. We promise not to touch, boss," Sage says.

"I don't want you to feel uncomfortable at work." He winks at her. "You know because you'd be harboring impure thoughts about the boss during working hours."

She licks her lips and lets her eyes roam up and down his body. "Who says I don't have impure thoughts about the boss now?"

Feather riffles through her purse and digs out a bunch of ones before waving them around. "And we'll pay you."

"I'm sorry to inform you the town ordinance forbids me from stripping for you lovely ladies." Ladies? They're practically eating him alive with their eyes. Aren't ladies supposed to be demure?

Everyone looks to Lilac for confirmation. "It's true. The Chief of Police is not allowed to earn any additional money other than his salary as police chief."

"This is some bull cocky." Feather throws her ones down on the floor.

Lyric tips his imaginary hat. "If you'll excuse me, I need to discuss something with the proprietor of this here establishment."

"Aspen and Lyric sitting in a tree. K-I—"

I growl and get in Ashlyn's face before she can continue. "Don't make me tell Rowan how you feel about him."

She gasps. "You wouldn't!"

"Don't test me."

Lyric squeezes my elbow and guides me out of the bookstore into the back storage area. As soon as the door closes behind us, I yank away from him.

"What do you need?"

"Need?" He scratches his jaw. "You appeared about ready to blow a gasket. I'm saving you."

My shoulders slump. "Sorry. I didn't mean to jump down your throat, but the women of this town drive me bonkers. When did they all become obsessed with sex?"

He chuckles. "They always have been. But they tend to keep it clean around the kids. You've just never lived here as an adult."

"Are they making out?" Ellery asks loud enough for us to hear her on the other side of the door.

"Your sisters on the other hand …" He doesn't finish his thought. He doesn't need to. I've always known how annoying my siblings are.

"You better leave before they figure out how the security cameras work."

"If you need me to rescue you, you have my number." He kisses my cheek and saunters out the back door with those sexy thighs on full display.

As I watch him saunter off, I realize avoiding Lyric is not going to be as easy as I originally thought. And that boy has trouble written all over him.

Chapter 18

Adventure – a daring experience. Note – it's not for everyone.

I DRAG THE LADDER over to the furthest corner of the back storage area of the bookstore. According to Saffron, there should be a box with books about the region around here somewhere. Since I'm now in charge of the tourist center for this town – whether I agreed to be or not doesn't seem to matter to the 'good' people of Winter Falls – I'm on the search for information.

I climb the ladder and move stuff around until I find an old box in the far back. I stand on my tiptoes to reach it, and the ladder wobbles. Uh oh. I hold my breath until it settles.

Once I'm confident I'm not going to plunge to my death in the back of a bookstore in my hometown – at least I don't have to worry about cats eating my face in this nosy town – I slide the box forward and a lifetime's worth of dust flies into the air.

Achoo. Achoo. Achoo.

I wait until the sneezing stops to try again. This time I manage to get the box in my hands without sounding like I'm having a hay fever attack. I don't even have hay fever.

I hug the box to my chest and begin climbing down the ladder. I'm nearly to the ground when the bottom of the box gives out and papers and books cascade to the floor. One book lands smack dab on my foot.

"Ow!" I screech and lift my foot to access the damage, but – dang it – I'm still standing on a ladder. I lose my balance and sway backwards. I claw at the ladder to steady myself, but I miss and stumble off.

"Double ow!"

I hobble on one foot, trying to regain my balance, until I hit the back wall with an *oof!* and slide to the floor.

Waffles opens one eye and tilts his head at me. He looks as if he's berating me for being so loud.

"It's not my fault," I tell him. "The book landed on my foot."

He chuffs as if to say *Hey, I'm trying to sleep here!* before closing his eyes to return to his nap.

"Thanks for your help, dog." This time he doesn't bother to respond.

I twist and turn my foot to check for injuries. Apart from a red mark where the book hit me, it appears fine. Time to test my theory. I stand and walk back and forth in the room to ensure my foot's in working order. Walking isn't painful and I have a full range of motion. No broken bones today.

Time to get back to work. I collect the items from the box that have scattered all over the room and gather everything into a pile before setting it on the table.

"Let's see what we have here."

There are a few copies of Old Man Mercury's book about the town. I examine them. They appear in good condition and, considering the vast amount of pictures sprinkled throughout the book, they should be decent sellers. I'll have to get in touch with Mercury to ask if he has more copies.

Other than the books, there are a bunch of papers – old inventory lists and newspapers I have no use for. I gather them into a pile for the recycling bin.

"Come on, lazybones. Time to go out."

Waffles yawns and stretches before deigning to join me on my journey to the recycling bin at the end of the alleyway. The trip must be a tough one since he goes straight back to sleep upon our return.

"Some of us have to work for a living," I grumble at him but get no response.

When I pick up the pile of Mercury's books to carry them to the front of the store, a slip of paper falls out and floats to the floor. I set the books down and kneel to examine the paper. It's probably another invoice for toilet paper from thirty years ago.

Huh. It's an envelope. The paper is brittle, and the address is illegible. But maybe I can make out the date stamped on it. Is that 1955?

I slide my finger along the seam of the envelope to open it. I squeal when I notice there's a letter inside.

"Isn't this exciting, Waffles?" He obviously doesn't agree as he continues to snore away in the corner. Someone's a lazy dog.

I allow the letter to fall out of the envelope onto the table. My fingers tremble in excitement but I force myself to slow down and carefully unfold the letter before I rip it in my enthusiasm.

My darling Robert,

By the time you receive this letter, I shall be on my way to you. I booked my journey with the Rock Island Line from Chicago to Denver. I shall arrive on March 9th.

Oh, how my heart longs to see you again. It has been two long and miserable years as I awaited word from you. I never doubted our love despite the cruel words uttered by my friends and family about you and your integrity. My faith in you remains steadfast and firm.

I pray the time flies until I am in your loving arms once again.

All my love.

Patiently yours,

Patricia

PS I hope you hid the money well.

"Hid the money well!"

I must have shouted as Waffles howls in response.

"Sorry, Waffles. Carry on with your nap. You poor thing. You only slept twelve hours today. I know you need your beauty rest." He yawns before settling back into his doggy bed proving Lilac isn't the only family member who doesn't understand sarcasm.

"Aspen!" Lyric calls out, and I scream as I jump to my feet.

He rushes through the door from the bookstore with his gun raised. He scans the room but after he confirms Waffles and I are alone, he holsters his weapon.

"Why did you scream?"

I rub my chest where my heart is beating out of control. "You scared me half to death."

He checks his watch. "I'm right on time."

Oops. In my excitement, I nearly forgot we're meeting tonight to discuss the Mabon Festival Parade.

"Sorry. I was preoccupied. You won't believe this." I grasp his hand and drag him to the table. "Read this."

He leans over the letter. "What am I reading?"

"It's a letter from 1955."

He shrugs. "It's a love letter. What's the big deal?"

I point to the postscript, being careful not to touch the letter itself. "Read the PS."

"I hope you hid the money well," he reads aloud. "I don't know what you're excited about."

"Don't you understand? It's a mystery!" I clap my hands.

"A mystery? What kind of mystery?"

"It could be anything. Maybe this guy is a money forger, or he robbed a railroad. Oh! He could have robbed a bank!"

"The statute of limitations on any crime committed in 1955 is expired by now unless there's a murder involved."

"A murder? Even more exciting!"

"I don't find murder exciting."

I roll my eyes. "That's Chief of Police Alston talking. May I speak to Lyric please?"

"We're one in the same person."

"No, you're not. Lyric's the guy who I caught skinny dipping at the falls. Chief Alston is the lawman who stopped Lennon from selling absinthe at *Electric Vibes*."

He blows out a puff of air. "Absinthe is seriously dangerous. It contains thujone which, in addition to the hallucinations Lennon is after, can cause seizures."

"Thank you for proving my point." When he gives me a blank look, I explain, "About how Chief Alston is boring."

He bends over to whisper in my ear. "I'll show you boring."

His breath wafts over my skin and goosebumps explode. His tongue peeks out and he swirls it against the skin behind my ear. I shiver and arch my neck to give him better access.

Woof! Woof!

Crap on a cracker! What am I doing?

I push Lyric away. "What are you doing?"

He smirks. "If I have to explain, I'm not doing it right."

"We're not picking up where we left off ten years ago."

"But now you know I'm not a cheater and I've forgiven you for deserting me."

What? He thinks I deserted him? I fist my hands on my hips. "Forgiven me?"

"I misspoke."

"I—" I cut myself off. *Stop this, Aspen.* I am not getting back together with Lyric no matter how sexy those thighs are. "It doesn't matter. We can't do this."

He steps closer and rests a hand on my hip. "As I recall, we *can* do this, and we're damn good at it, too."

My nipples tingle, and I sway toward him. "I'm not here long-term, remember?"

"Nothing says we can't have a good time until you leave."

Wrong. I could barely drive away from him the first time I left town. How will I drive away from him again? I won't. I can't. No one is strong enough to drive away from this man twice. There's only one way to be certain I return to Dallas where I've built up my life – stay away from this man.

I step back. "I don't think it's a good idea."

"I think it's a fantastic idea, but I will respect your wishes."

His words say one thing, but the sparkle in his blue eyes tells me I need to watch out because he'll force his way through any opening – no matter how minuscule – I give him.

"Thank you. Now, shall we get to work on the preparation for the Mabon Festival Parade? Despite knowing the good people of this town threw this project at us because they're trying to shove us together – stupid Project Weston – I plan to do the best job I possibly can."

"They'd stop with their matchmaking shenanigans if we went out on a date."

"You're like a dog with a bone. Now, can you tell me what exactly I need to do?"

He stares at me for a long moment before responding, "Yep."

Phew. He's not going to push this whole dating thing. I'm not stupid. He'll ask me out again. I just need to make sure I'm not alone with him again until my plans to return to Dallas are set in stone. Should be easy. Assuming the entire town doesn't gang up on me. Maybe not so easy then.

Chapter 19

Ding-dong ditch – not a harmless prank when you're met with a shotgun at the door

"WAIT! WHERE ARE YOU going? Aren't we going to Rowan's to get a treat?" Ellery asks when I drive straight past *Bake Me Happy*.

Now I've got her confined to the golf cart – although technically at the speeds we're allowed to drive, she could easily jump out – I tell her.

"Old Man Mercury's."

"What?" she screeches. "Are you out of your mind? His house is haunted."

I roll my eyes. "His house isn't haunted." I pause. "Okay, maybe it is, but this is an adventure."

"You and your adventures. I'm surprised you didn't put on your hobbit feet and make me call you Bilbo."

"I dressed up as Bilbo for one Halloween. One! When are you going to stop teasing me about it?"

She snorts. "Never, nerd."

Time to move on. "Guess what I found in the storage room at *Fall Into a Good Book*."

She rubs her hands together. "Let me think. A witches' potion?"

"A witches' potion? Where did you come up with such an idea?"

"If not a potion, what about a Ouija board? Even better – a moving Ouija board."

"Since when do you have this obsession with the occult?"

"You said we're going on an adventure and we're going to a haunted house. One plus one equals occult."

"No occult."

"Fine," she huffs. "What about a treasure map? No, wait. What about a box full of money? Lots and lots of money!"

"You're getting warmer."

She claps her hands. "Tell me! Tell me!"

"I found an old letter in a box and ..." I pause for dramatic effect.

Ellery slaps me. "Don't be a drama llama. Tell me!"

"It's a love letter, but it refers to and I quote here 'hiding the money'."

"Holy guacamole! This *is* an adventure."

"Told you so."

"Lilac, Juniper, and Ashlyn are going to be mad you didn't invite them to come with us."

"Lilac? Really?"

"She loves a good mystery. 'Science' is one big mystery to be solved, according to her."

"And yet you think I'm the nerd?"

"Do I need to show you your ninth grade school picture again?"

I cringe. Ninth grade was a bad year for me. Glasses, braces, and out of control curly hair are not attractive at any age.

I turn into the driveway of Old Man Mercury's house and slow the golf cart to a near crawl. As kids, we were convinced his house was haunted. We would dare each other to sneak through his yard with its knee-high weeds and climb the rotted stairs and porch to ring his doorbell.

Lyric was the only one who didn't chicken out and actually made it to the door. But when he was greeted with a shotgun, it was game over. Our parents forbade us from bothering poor old Mercury.

At the time, I thought he was a crotchety old man. Now, I'm wondering what his tragic story is, and if he'll write about it for me.

"I hope he doesn't still have that shotgun," Ellery says as she studies the house.

"It'll be fine. He's not going to shoot us in broad daylight." I hope.

We reach the end of the driveway and I pull the golf cart to a stop in front of his porch. The porch steps appear to be as rotten as they were twenty years ago. Someone didn't get the memo from the town beautification committee.

Before we can get out of the golf cart, Mercury's door opens, and he steps out.

"I was wondering how long it would be before you landed at my door," he yells.

"How did you know we were coming?" I ask as I stand at the bottom of the stairs.

Anyone else in Winter Falls, I'd invite myself in. But here? I'm not taking any chances.

"You're in charge of the town tourist center. I figure you want some more of those books I wrote on the history of the town."

"I do, but there's another reason I came here today."

He growls. "I am not playing the grim reaper at the Mabon Festival Parade."

I hold my palms up. "I wouldn't ask you." Although, he would make an awesome grim reaper with his slim build and pale, gaunt face.

He glares at me. "I know you and that young pup Lyric are in charge of the parade."

"How do you know about the parade?" He wasn't at the town meeting.

"I'm old, not a hermit." Could have fooled me. "I read the town's Facebook page." Gossip page is the word I'd use to describe it.

"I'm here about something else." I pause.

"Well, what about? I ain't got all day."

He doesn't? What does he do with his time?

"I found a letter in the back of the bookstore. It's from 1955."

"Why didn't you say so in the first place?" he says before turning around and returning inside his house.

Ellery leans over and whispers, "Are we supposed to follow him?"

"Are you coming or what?"

"I guess we are," she mutters before shoving me in front of her. "You're older. You should sacrifice yourself for me."

"Scaredy-cat."

I try to make my words sound brave, but my hands tremble as I climb the stairs to Mercury's porch while being careful to avoid the rotten boards. Ellery grabs the back of my shirt and follows me. The porch creaks as we tiptoe across it.

The boards are old and rotten, Aspen. It's nothing to be afraid of.

I nudge the screen door, and it squeaks as it opens. I take a deep breath and remind myself I am not a coward. If I can jump off the falls into the river bare ass naked in the middle of winter, I can do this. I force myself to enter the house.

I pause to allow my eyes to adjust to the dark inside the house. Outside it's a sunny summer day, but in here it's dark and cool. Are haunted houses cold or warm?

"You going to stand in my doorway all day?" Mercury barks and I jump.

This is ridiculous, Aspen. He's a man, not a ghost or monster. Get yourself together, girl.

I shove Ellery off of me and stride to the kitchen where Mercury's waiting for us. There's a jug of lemonade and glasses on the table.

"You pour. My old arthritic hands aren't too steady anymore."

Ellery and I sit next to each other, and I pour lemonade for everyone.

"How are—"

"I ain't got time for no gossiping. You mentioned a letter."

I open my bag and retrieve the transparent folder I placed the letter in to protect it. I set it on the table and slide it across to Mercury.

Mercury frowns, but he takes the letter and quickly scans it. When he finishes and looks up at me, his eyes are sparkling.

"I'll be damned. It's always been rumored the loot was hidden somewhere near Winter Falls, but this proves it."

"Loot? What loot? What rumors?"

"You don't know the story?"

I shake my head.

He smiles. "In 1955, the Hastings National Bank in Hastings, Nebraska was robbed of approximately fifty-thousand dollars by a solo bank robber. The robber was rumored to be the Black Hat Bandit. Local legend has it the Black Hat Bandit jumped on the Union Pacific Railroad and made his way from Nebraska to Colorado to a spot not far from here."

"I thought there wasn't anything here when the town was settled in 1960?"

"Except for the old mansion," Ellery says.

Mercury pursues his lips. "Had you read my book, you'd know there was a small settlement here before Winter Falls was established. The town settlers offered the former inhabitants compensation to move."

"Sorry." Geez. I guess I should read his book.

"As I was saying, the Black Hat Bandit made his way to this area and sent word to his beloved to join him."

"Patricia!"

He nods. "Yes, Patricia. But she never made it here."

I lean closer. "What happened?"

"There was a railroad crash somewhere in Kansas and most of the people aboard died."

I gasp. "Patricia died?"

"Best as I can figure out, she did."

"And what happened to the Black Hat Bandit?" Ellery asks.

Mercury scratches his beard. "He was caught trying to rob a bank in Oklahoma. He admitted to robbing the Hastings National Bank, but he never would tell anyone where he hid the money."

My eyes widen as I consider the implications of what he said. "You mean there could be fifty-thousand dollars from a bank robbery hidden somewhere in town?"

He shrugs. "Or in the hills somewhere. Who knows where a bank robber would hide his loot?"

"But it must have remained hidden," Ellery points out.

"Why do you think it's still hidden?"

"There's no way someone found fifty-thousand dollars cash, and no one knows about it. Do you know how much it would be worth in today's money? Probably around half a million."

I'm certain my eyes are the size of saucers now. "There's half a million dollars hidden somewhere near here?"

"I always reckoned the Black Hat Bandit stopped here. The mansion owner bragged about having met him before he passed, but this letter…" He taps the letter. "Proves I was right."

"You want to help us find the money?" I ask him. I figure we'll need his help considering neither Ellery nor I had heard the story before.

"I'm too old to go out treasure hunting but come back anytime if you have questions."

An open invitation from Old Man Mercury? And the surprises keep on coming.

Ellery and I stand. "Thank you, Mercury. It's been a pleasure visiting with you today." Except for when I nearly peed myself in fright.

"See yourself out. These old bones don't move so well anymore."

Ellery and I don't speak as we set off in the golf cart. As soon as we're back on the main road, though, I pull to the side and squeal, "We're going on an adventure!"

"We better bring in Lilac, Juniper, and Ashlyn or we'll never hear the end of it."

"The more the merrier," I sing as I switch on the golf cart and drive toward town.

And here I thought my time back in my hometown would be boring. *Did you forget about Lyric?* A small voice in my head whispers but I ignore it. Fun with Lyric is not on the menu.

Chapter 20

Hometown – the place where everyone knows all the embarrassing things you did as a kid

"And there you have it," Lyric says and shuts his notebook.

I stare at him. "Are you serious?"

We're meeting to discuss the Mabon Festival Parade since our last meeting didn't go very well. Someone – spoiler alert: it was me – was too excited about finding the letter from Patricia to discuss anything remotely involved in a parade.

"Why didn't you tell me this meeting was a waste of time?"

He cocks an eyebrow. "Would you have believed me?"

"Yes."

"Liar," he accuses, and I shrug since I am lying. But white lies are perfectly acceptable when your ex is involved. I'm positive it's written down in the rules somewhere.

My tummy rumbles, and I feel my face heat.

Lyric chuckles. "Come on. I'll treat you to dinner at the diner."

I want to say I'll go home and eat, but my stomach rumbles again. "Fine. But it's not a date."

He places his hand on his chest and gives me his 'innocent' look. Innocent? The man hasn't been innocent for over fifteen years. I should know. I was there when he lost his innocence. In fact, I was an active participant.

I roll my eyes. "Let's go before I change my mind and decide to brave no meat Tuesday at home."

"Your mother is a wonderful cook."

"Still kissing the principal's ass after all these years? She can't give you detention anymore."

"Maybe not, but she can ask me to paint the entire outside of the school at a town meeting."

I giggle. "Glad to hear I'm not the only one who's been railroaded at a town meeting."

"There's an ongoing wager on who'll be the next 'victim' each month."

Betting is a town pastime. "Some things never change."

"There's a reason Lennon opened a concession stand at the meetings."

I groan. "Don't remind me. I'm not eighteen anymore. Drinking three beers in the space of an hour is not fun."

"You better work on your tolerance. Ashlyn picks a different word for each meeting."

"My sister is a troublemaker."

He bumps my shoulder. "All the West girls are troublemakers."

"I don't know what you're talking about. I'm an angel."

"You're a ray of sunshine."

"Exactly."

He opens the door to the diner and all chatter in the place comes to a halt. A few people exchange money as well. Stupid townspeople and their betting.

"We're not on a date!"

Several people sigh before money is once again exchanged. "Thanks a lot, Aspen! You're costing me a fortune."

I wave at Petal. "I told you I didn't need those sex candles."

"Aspen Cloud West and Lyric Journey Alston, as I live and breath. It's like old times," the owner of the diner, Gracious, greets us before trying to squeeze me to death in a hug.

"Can't breathe."

Lyric saves me from the Gracious hug of death. "What? No hug for me?"

She slaps his chest. "You charmer, you."

Gracious shows us to a booth in the middle of the row next to the window. Great. In addition to all the people in the diner being able to watch us, everyone strolling past on Main Street can, too. The rumor mill will be going into overdrive tonight.

"Let me guess, Aspen wants the club sandwich and sweet potato fries with a strawberry milkshake, and Lyric will have a burger with potato fries and a coke."

"I haven't had a strawberry milkshake in forever."

Gracious winks at me. "Then, it will taste all the much sweeter," she says and saunters off.

"I'm going to have to start running again with all the food the people in this town feed me."

Lyric waggles his brows. "I think you're gorgeous. I always did love your curves."

Someone behind me sighs, and I turn around to glare at her. "No encouraging him, Sage."

Love Hill struts by. "Girl, he's going to need all the encouragement he can get to want the chubby four-eyed girl."

I snort. Does she think she can bully me? If she couldn't bully me in high school, she has zero chance now.

I point to my eyes. "Not four eyes anymore. Laser surgery."

"I miss those sexy, librarian glasses you used to wear."

Love grunts at his comment before stomping off.

I giggle. "You could just tell her you're not interested."

"I'm serious. Please tell me you kept a pair of those black-rimmed glasses. I loved removing those."

"I bet your glasses aren't the only thing he loved removing," Sage mumbles behind me.

I stand and march to her table. When I notice she's done eating, I scan the area until I spot the gray busser's tub. I snatch it before proceeding to clear Sage's table. I throw all her dirty dishes in the tub, including the half-full glass of coke.

"You can pay at the counter." I stare her down until she stands.

"You used to be fun, Aspen Cloud."

"And you used to not be such a busybody."

She snorts. "Wrong."

Once she leaves, I glare at the other customers in the diner. "Who else needs their table bussed?"

Suddenly, everyone in the place finds the table tops super interesting. I wait a moment, but no one will lift their head and meet my gaze. Alrighty then. I march back to my seat.

"It's not funny," I snarl at Lyric who's sporting a big fat smile on his face.

"I don't remember you being this worried about gossip before."

"Yeah, well, the gossip was usually correct back in the day, although how everyone knew about the waterfall incident before I made it home remains a mystery to me."

"Probably because all the lights in town flickered when you hit the pole. My dad was not amused. He grounded me for life."

I waggle my eyebrows. "Didn't stop you from sneaking out to my house the next night."

He grins. "Do your parents still have the treehouse?"

"You know it. Apparently, I'm a 'bad' example since all my sisters used the treehouse for their romantic encounters."

"Bad example? Your mother would never think you're a bad example when it comes to sex. She literally handed me condoms the first time I picked you up for a date. We were fifteen."

"Mom and her obsession with safe sex." Sigh. "I was a bad example because the treehouse was uncomfortable with no real bed."

"I love your mom, but there was no way I was having sex with you in their house, especially since someone's a screamer."

My mouth drops open. How dare he! "I am not a screamer."

"What's wrong with a screamer?" Gracious asks as she sets our food on the table. "You know you're getting it good when you scream."

I groan and drop my head to the table.

"Aspen Cloud West, do not tell me you've turned into a prude living in the big city!"

"Thanks for shouting," I mumble to the table before sitting up. "I think the people at the other end of Main Street didn't hear you."

"It's a good thing you're back home. We need to cure you of those big city evils."

I open my mouth to remind her I'm not home for good, but she doesn't give me a chance to respond.

"Now, eat your food, and don't you dare say anything about getting fat. You're all skin and bones."

"Skin and bones," I whisper once she's gone. "Did she miss my giant caboose when I walked in?"

"I happen to find your caboose sexy."

"Shaddap. Not a date, remember?"

He grunts. "I think the whole town remembers."

I'm not having this argument again. I concentrate on my food instead. I bite into the club sandwich and moan. No one makes a club sandwich the way Gracious does. The bacon is the perfect crispness, and she uses some spicy mayonnaise I've tried for years to replicate without success.

When I look across the table, Lyric is staring at me with fire in his eyes. "If you don't want this to be a date, you can't moan."

"Is this a strict rule? No moaning at all or no moaning when I'm eating."

"Oh, Sunshine. You can moan all you want when I—"

I hold up my hand. "Enough! I don't remember you being this stubborn."

"Chief Alston, not stubborn?" Petal asks as she passes by. "He made us do a sit-in for three days before he gave in on the gas station. Do you know how hard it is for someone of my age to sit on the hard ground for three days?"

"As I recall, you brought a camping chair with you and a bunch of candles."

"Which Mr. Stubborn wouldn't let me light."

"I wasn't having you light fifty candles for a candlelight vigil for the end of the earth. You would have burned down the station."

Orion grunts behind his wife. "I can't tell you how many times we've had to replace the curtains in the bedroom because of those damn candles."

"Damn candles? You never seem to complain when I'm pouring the paraffin on you."

Pouring the paraffin on him? Yikes. I don't need to know about their sex life. A subject change is in order.

"You should consider frosted glass instead. It eliminates the need for drapes," I suggest.

Petal claps. "Wonderful idea. And a great excuse to re-decorate the bedroom. Come on, slow poke. Pinterest waits for no woman."

Orion sighs as he follows her out of the diner.

"The townspeople haven't given up on sit-ins?"

"Hell no. I had to designate a special area of the town hall for them."

"I love how everyone in this town not only has strong principles, but they stand up for their convictions. They think one person can make a difference."

I sip on my strawberry milkshake and notice Lyric's staring at me again.

"What? I didn't groan." I check my top for spillage. "Didn't spill either."

"Which is kind of a miracle considering it's you." I stick my tongue out at him. "I'm just coming to realize how much you love this town despite all the bitching you do about it."

I open my mouth to tell him … I don't know what, to be honest. Yes, I love my hometown. It doesn't mean I want to live here, though. Although, it is awful nice how everyone knows your name. Plus, it's safe and quirky.

Oh shit. Do I want to move back? Nope. I am shoving those thoughts right out of my mind. I am not moving back. No, sirree bob. Not happening.

Chapter 21

Step – how every journey of a thousand miles begins

LYRIC

I whistle as I stroll up the sidewalk to the West house. Mrs. West invited me for Sunday lunch today, but I'm fairly certain she hasn't told Aspen. I always did like Aspen's mom.

Ashlyn opens the door and smirks. "Mom! Your surprise guest has arrived."

Mrs. West rushes up behind her. "No need to scream the house down. Let him in, baby cakes."

Ashlyn rolls her eyes and turns to leave. I guess she's not letting me in.

"Ignore her, Lyric. I swear somedays it's like she never grew out of her teenage phase."

I smile and hand her the gift I brought. "This is for you."

"Is this a semi-cactus dahlia?" I nod. "Good job! This single-flower dahlia is a pollinator, and you do know how much I love my pollinators."

I have no response since I can barely remember what a pollinator is from high school biology.

"Why are you still standing out there? Come in. Come in."

I follow her into the dining room where Ellery is setting the table. "Aspen is going to lose her mind," she remarks.

"You do know you can't actually lose your mind, don't you?" Lilac asks as she joins us.

Juniper shushes her. "Quiet. I hear big sis coming down the stairs now."

The four sisters scramble into the kitchen, leaving me all alone in the dining room when Aspen enters. She takes one look at me and yells, "Mom!"

"Is that any way to greet your gentleman caller?" Juniper asks from her position in the kitchen where she's eavesdropping.

"Gentleman caller? Does this mean you finally read *The Glass Menagerie*?"

"I saw the movie years ago."

Aspen grunts. "As if a movie can compare to the original Tennessee Williams play."

"My book nerd is alive and well."

She frowns at me before shouting, "Mom," again.

"Mom's not here," Ashlyn says.

"Yes, she is. She's right here in the kitchen," Lilac counters. "Ouch! Why did you pinch me? You know the rules. If you expect me to lie, you need to tell me in advance."

"Lilac hasn't changed one bit."

"What does he mean? Was there a tone? Is this sarcasm?"

I chuckle. "You might as well come out."

The kitchen door swings open and Ashlyn, Juniper, Lilac, and Ellery trudge into the dining room.

"Aspen is boring. When my gentleman caller comes, I'm going to show him how happy I am to see him," Ashlyn declares.

I lean close to whisper to Aspen, "Is she talking about Rowan?"

At her nod, I frown. Rowan and Ashlyn together is never going to happen. I happen to know Rowan thinks he'd be robbing the cradle since he's eight years older than Ashlyn.

"Don't you dare pity me, Mr. Can't Get a Date with My Sister," Ashlyn hisses at me.

I know better than to respond to her pissed off tone. I raise my hands in surrender.

Mrs. West bustles in. "I don't know why not. He and Aspen were inseparable as teenagers. I don't know how many times I had to replace the screen on her bedroom window."

Aspen gasps. "You knew about me sneaking out?"

Her mom rolls her eyes. "Naturally. A mother always knows. Why do you think you kept finding condoms in your backpack?"

Aspen's face darkens. "We didn't have sex every single time I snuck out."

"You didn't? Why for goodness sakes not?"

The sliding door opens and Mr. West rambles inside. He kisses his wife and pats her on her rear before glancing around and noticing me. "Hey, Lyric. I didn't know you'd be joining us today."

"Because you can't keep a secret any better than our middle child can lie."

"I'm positive the refusal to lie is a virtue," Lilac points out.

"Since when is the word virtue in your vocabulary?" Aspen asks her.

"I told you. Sociology is fascinating."

Mrs. West claps her hands. "Let's sit down, shall we? Lyric you're in your old spot next to Aspen."

There's no doubt in my mind she uses the phrase 'old spot' on purpose to remind Aspen yet again of how good we used to be together. And all I can say to her is 'keep up the good work, Mrs. West'. I know better than to say those words out loud, though, and wink at her instead.

Everyone sits and I slide my chair as close as possible to Aspen's. She glares at me, but she has nowhere to go, and we both know it.

I lean over and kiss her cheek. "Hello, Sunshine."

"Are you trying to encourage Mrs. Matchmaker?" Of course, I am. "Never mind. Your smirk is answer enough."

"The food smells delicious, Mrs. West."

I'm not lying. The pot roast and roasted vegetables smell mouth-watering especially since I haven't had a homemade meal in a while with my parents on their excursion to 'find themselves'. I didn't realize they were lost.

"Suck up," Aspen says out of the corner of her mouth. I wink at her in response.

Mrs. West sighs. "Such a lovely couple. And you," she uses her fork to point at me, "you're old enough to call me Ruby and Aspen's father, Daniel."

"Are you done with the matchmaking, or can I ask Aspen a question?" Daniel asks. Ruby glares at him, but he doesn't pay her any mind.

"Yeah, Mom. Are you done with the matchmaking yet?" Aspen mimics.

"Are you married or pregnant?"

"Pregnant? We haven't... we're not... it's not," Aspen sputters.

"I don't know why not," Lilac cuts her off to say, and I decide she's my favorite West sister, aside from Aspen of course.

"May I be excused?" Aspen asks.

Her mom purses her lips in response and Aspen's shoulders slump. She's not going anywhere.

"You haven't told me about your phone call with the insurance company yet," Daniel says and Aspen sighs.

"They said they'll need more time to evaluate the claim unless I accept the settlement. It's the same rigmarole they've been giving for weeks now."

My heart squeezes at how defeated she sounds. I'm happy to have her here in town, but I'm not happy about the circumstances. She lost everything in the fire, and the insurance company is still dragging its feet.

I find her thigh and squeeze. When she places her hand on top of mine, I know she must be more upset than she's letting on. She'd never accept my comfort without fighting me otherwise. But accepting my comfort when she needs it the most? Maybe there's hope for us yet.

"You need a lawyer," Daniel says.

"Let me guess. You know a good one."

He puffs out his chest. "As a matter of fact."

"I'll think about it."

"You won't believe what this guest said to me this morning," Ellery begins, and Aspen mouths *thank you* to her.

The rest of the meal is spent listening to Ellery tell tales from her inn. I smile and nod at all the appropriate times, but my mind is preoccupied with the news of Aspen's insurance company. Does this mean she's staying in town longer? If so, her excuse for not accepting a date from me is getting awful thin.

"Aspen, why don't you escort Lyric home?" her mom suggests once we've polished off her rhubarb pie.

"It's still light out, and he's the Chief of Police. He'll be perfectly safe walking home in Winter Falls by himself."

Ruby yanks her oldest daughter to her feet and shoves a container holding another rhubarb pie in Aspen's hands before spinning her around and propelling her to the door.

"It's the polite thing to do," she insists as she opens the door and shoves Aspen outside.

Once we're on the porch, Aspen stares at the closed door. "What just happened? Did my mother kick me out of my own home?"

"I didn't kick you out," Ruby yells from the other side of the door. "You're welcome back in an hour."

"An hour? A snail can make it to Lyric's house and back in less time!"

"No, it can't," Juniper shouts. "Snails don't move more than three feet per hour."

I relieve Aspen of the container and wrap my arm around her shoulders.

"Come on. Protect me on my way home."

She elbows me. "Why? You've never needed protecting before."

"Oh, but I have. Don't you remember the time in sixth grade when you punched Love Hill for teasing me?"

Her eyes widen. "I didn't think you remembered I was the one who punched her."

I start toward my house, dragging her along with me. "Of course, I remember. I remember everything about you."

She snorts. "You didn't know I existed until my boobs arrived."

"I knew you existed," I insist.

"Whatever."

We walk the rest of the way to my house in silence. The trip is over entirely too quickly since I live less than ten minutes from the West family house. This is Winter Falls. You can get anywhere in the town in less than ten minutes.

Aspen sighs as she gazes up at my place. "I always loved this house."

I know. It's the reason I bought the place all those years ago when she first left town. I thought owning the house she'd always dreamed of having would help convince her to return home. But then she ghosted me and— I slam the door on those thoughts. It's the past. I'm looking to the future. And the future starts now.

I set the pie down on my porch and grab Aspen's hands.

"Aspen Cloud West, do you want to go out on a date with me?"

Her nose scrunches. "I thought we agreed we wouldn't date."

"I don't remember agreeing to such a crazy idea."

"I'm not here forever, remember?"

"But you are here until the insurance company is done with their investigation and who knows how long it will take since they're obviously dragging their feet."

I've never been so happy for someone to be caught up in the mechanizations of a corporation before. I should probably feel guilty for how they're treating Aspen, but there's no need when it's obvious how happy she is to be home.

She puffs out a breath of air. "You're like a dog with a bone."

"Woof!"

She rolls her eyes. "Fine. I'll go out on with you on one condition."

"Name it."

"It's one date and one date only. Afterwards, there will be no more asking me out."

I use her hands to draw her near. "Unless I can change your mind."

"You won't."

"Challenge accepted," I whisper before my head descends and I allow my lips to touch hers for a brief moment.

I step back before I decide to hell with it and drag her into my house to have my way with her. Her eyes are dilated, and she's panting for breath. I wouldn't need to work very hard to convince her to come inside. But I don't want her to come inside for one night. No, I want forever with this woman.

I bop her nose. "Be safe getting home, Sunshine."

Chapter 22

Recreate – re-enact a moment in time in order to remind a person how good those times were

"Your date's here," Ashlyn shouts from downstairs.

"Why are you here? You don't live here," I shout back down to her.

I don't hear her answer. I'm too busy staring at myself in the mirror. This outfit – a short skirt and wraparound top – screams 'date'. Yeah, yeah. I know I'm going on a date, but I don't want Lyric to get any ideas of where this non-relationship is going.

Mom sticks her head in my room. "You're beautiful, baby girl."

I roll my eyes. Mom said I was beautiful when I had buck teeth and thick glasses. Her opinion is not to be trusted.

"Don't make him wait. All of your sisters are here." With her parting shot fired, she leaves.

Crap. I can't leave Lyric downstairs with my sisters. I grab a sweater and my purse before rushing down the stairs. When I arrive in the living room, it's to find all four of my sisters sitting on the sofa grilling Lyric like they haven't known him their entire lives.

"And what do you do for work, Mr. Alston?" Ellery asks.

Lyric smiles. "Call me Lyric. I want to be a police officer."

"Want to be a police officer?" Lilac asks. "I'm confused. Is he not the Chief of Police?"

Juniper elbows her. "And you'll treat my sister properly. You won't try to take advantage of my big sis, will you?"

Lyric plays along. "No ma'am, I won't."

"Here you go." Mom hands him a condom. "Just in case."

He blushes as he places the condom in his back pocket.

"Ahem. Maybe we should get going," I suggest.

"Here. This is for you." He hands me a pot containing several flower bulbs.

"Thank you."

Mom takes the pot from me and nudges me toward the door. "Have a nice evening."

"Thank you, Mrs. West."

We step outside. Lyric places his hand on my lower back and leads me toward a golf cart.

"Your parent's golf cart? Why do we need a golf cart? Where are we going?" My stomach rumbles. "I assumed we'd have dinner."

"Don't worry. I'll feed the monster in your stomach." He clears his throat. "We're going to the diner."

"Then why did you bring the golf cart?" The diner is five minutes from my parent's house. There's no need for a golf cart. Wait a minute. Flower bulbs. His parent's golf car. The diner.

"You dork. Are you re-creating our first date?"

"Yep. I want to start over. And what better way to begin again than recreating the moment when you fell in love with me?"

"I didn't fall in love with you on our first date."

"Of course not." He winks. "You already loved me."

I glare at him because he's right. The jerk.

"Do you want to have this argument here where your entire family is watching and listening? Or shall we go to the diner?"

I peek over my shoulder and, sure enough, my sisters are peering out the front window at us.

"You're lucky you have brothers," I grumble as he helps me into the cart.

"Brothers can be annoying, too. Trust me."

"Your brothers have never embarrassed you in front of me."

He cocks an eyebrow. "They haven't? Don't tell me you forgot the time they pulled my pants down at the pep rally."

I giggle. Great memory. "How are River and Phoenix anyway? I haven't seen much of them since I've been back."

"Phoenix is still more in love with goats than people, and River is giving green tours to tourists. He wants to talk to you about advertising his business at the tourist center."

I groan. "I can't believe I got wrangled into creating a tourist center."

"It was your idea," he points out before parking the golf cart in front of the diner. "Stay there," he orders before rushing around the cart to help me out.

"I think I can manage," I complain, but I allow him to take my hand.

I glance through the window into the diner and note the place is packed. On top of which, I know every single person in the place. I tug on Lyric's hand to stop him.

"What's wrong?"

"Nothing. It's sweet you want to recreate our first date, but I really had my heart set on eating at the brewery. I've never been there before." I lay it on thick because I am not going inside the diner and having everyone there observe our date while the rest of the town gets a play-by-play thanks to social media.

"Your wish is my command."

We walk down Main Street to the other side of the square where the brewery is located. *Naked Falls Brewing* is new. Two out-of-towners arrived in Winter Falls three years ago and declared their intention to begin a brewery with a restaurant.

Usually, only long-term residents of Winter Falls are allowed to set up businesses on Main Street, but the strangers managed to win over the townspeople. Two years later, *Naked Falls Brewing* is not only up and running, but another tourist destination in town.

Lyric opens the door and ushers me inside.

"Wow. This place is pretty cool."

The building used to house the local newspaper. The owners kept the old brick walls and exposed the ductwork to give the place an industrial vibe.

We choose a table on the second-floor mezzanine where we can view all the happenings at the bar on the first floor. A waitress approaches us as soon as we sit down.

"Hey, Chief Alston." She greets him before smiling at me. "And this must be Aspen."

Sigh. This is small-town living. Everyone knows your name, even when you don't know them.

"Hi!" I wave. "Have we met?"

"You wouldn't remember me. I'm Moon. I was in the same class as Ashlyn. The last time you saw me I was wearing pigtails and hadn't grown these yet." She points to her chest area.

I narrow my eyes on her. "Weren't you Ashlyn's friend who followed me and Lyric around and tried to catch us when we went skinny dipping at the falls?"

She laughs. "It took me a month to stop itching from the poison ivy."

Someone shouts Moon's name. "Hold your horses," she snarls at the table before asking us, "You guys ready to order?"

We order two beers she recommends and some potato skins to tide us over until I have a chance to study the menu.

Lyric reaches across the table to grasp my hand. "I can't believe you remember those girls sneaking up on us when we were at the falls."

"It's awful hard to forget your sister falling into a bed of poison ivy."

"And you wouldn't help her out."

"Hello! I was naked."

His eyes flare. "I remember."

Dang him. Now, I'm remembering him naked that day. Then, he was a tall and lean teenager. I can tell from the way his t-shirt clings to his chest and biceps, he's filled out since. I bite my lip as I imagine how it would feel to get my hands on those muscles.

Moon plops our beer and appetizers down on the table and the mood is broken. Phew. *No more naked thoughts of Lyric, Aspen.* I sip at my beer to cool myself down.

"Do you remember the time we borrowed your parent's golf cart to drive to Denver for a concert?" Lyric asks.

"How could I forget? It was Pearl Jam. And we never made it to the concert."

"What made us think we could drive a golf cart over a hundred miles?"

"I blame your brother River. He's the one who said we could make it."

"I can't believe he majored in engineering at college."

"He knew the whole time we'd never make it, the little shit."

We spend the next hours reminiscing and catching up. We may have seen each other here and there over the years when I've been back home visiting, but we haven't actually talked. I wasn't about to talk to Mr. Cheater Cheater Pumpkin Eater and apparently, he was holding a grudge against me for abandoning him.

Moon stops at our table. "Last call."

Last call? Where did the time go?

"We should probably get going. I have to open the bookstore in a few hours."

"And I'm on duty tomorrow."

I reach for my purse, but Lyric stops me. "I'm paying."

"You—"

"I paid for our first date and I'm paying for this date."

"Are we back to recreating our first date again?"

"You guys are adorable," Moon says.

Crap. Our conversation and how Lyric tried to recreate our first date will be all over town before we're out of the restaurant.

Lyric holds out his hand. "Come on, Aspen. Let me escort you home."

We leave the golf cart in front of the diner and walk to my parent's house.

"I had a great time," I say when we stop on the sidewalk in front of my house.

"Don't sound so surprised."

I shrug. I am surprised. I guess I forgot how much fun Lyric and I used to have. Probably because I forced those memories out of my mind when I thought he betrayed me.

He cradles my face with his hands. "I'm going to kiss you now."

My breathing speeds up and my heart races. "Do you always announce when you're going to kiss someone?"

"Only for you, smartass. Only for you."

His head descends slowly, giving me a chance to pull away, but I couldn't pull away now if I wanted to and I don't want to. I want to feel his lips on mine more than I want my next breath.

His lips finally meet mine and I sigh. He uses the opportunity to push his tongue into my mouth and his taste explodes on my tongue. How have I survived this long without his lips on mine?

He groans and his hands move to wrap around me and drag me close until my breasts are squashed against his chest. My nipples harden at the feel of those hard muscles I've been fantasizing about touching.

Touching? Why are my hands are dangling like useless appendages when I could be touching Lyric instead? I'm not letting this opportunity pass me by. I wrap my arms around his waist and let one hand glide lower until I can feel his tight ass. I squeeze and he moans.

Lyric yanks his mouth away from mine and I mewl.

"Go out on another date with me?"

What? Why is he talking? Why aren't his lips on mine where they should be?

"Whatever. More kissing. Less talking."

I can feel the smile on his lips when they meet mine, but I don't care. I've probably signed up for heartbreak, but I'll worry about it tomorrow. Right now, I'm busy with other things.

Chapter 23

Nosy – prying into someone's personal affairs even when it's none of your dang business

"Hi! Can you show me how to research newspapers from the 1950s?" I ask Gratitude, the librarian.

I'm at the library to research the bank robbery Old Man Mercury told me about. I need to fact check his story before I begin my treasure hunt, although I have no idea how to actually conduct a treasure hunt. Who cares? It's an adventure. Part of the fun of an adventure is figuring things out.

"Don't be silly, I'll help you."

I whirl around at Lilac's declaration. "What are you doing here?"

"We're here to help you find the loot!" Ashlyn shouts.

I shush her. "Do you want everyone to know about the money?"

She scans the library. "There's no one here."

It's true. The library isn't exactly bustling with people since it's August and the schools are out for summer. But Ashlyn knows news travels faster than wildfire in this town. Even if no one's here right now, someone will find out what we're doing. Small towns are kind of amazing that way.

"Come along." Lilac leads us to the microfiche room. "Before the internet exploded, there were these things called newspapers."

"Yeah, Ms. Know It All, we know. The *Winter Falls Post* used to be located in the building where the brewery is now," I say.

"Isn't the brewery where Lyric took you on a date?" Ellery asks.

"I thought we were here to research the bank robbery."

"I agree," Lilac says, and I could kiss her. "We'll discuss Aspen's pathetic love live after we finish our research." There goes her kiss.

"But why would the local newspaper print an article about a robbery in another state?" Ellery asks the question I'm thinking.

"I'm not researching the *Winter Falls Post*. It wasn't established until 1960. And didn't you say the robbery of the Hastings National Bank occurred in 1955?"

"According to Mercury."

"The microfiche collection contains various newspapers from the region. I'm theorizing a bank robbery one state over in Nebraska would be big news here in Colorado as well. One of the local newspapers must have reported about it," Lilac explains as she opens a file drawer.

Ellery, Juniper, Ashlyn, and I watch as Lilac goes to work. She removes several boxes of microfiche before sitting down in front of the scanner and starting to review them.

"Holy cow! Is she actually reading? No one can read that fast." Juniper points to the scanner where the microfiche whirls past at a speed faster than humans can see, let alone read.

"I'm scanning the headlines," Lilac mumbles. "Hold on. I think I have something."

We crowd around the scanner. "Here." she points to an article, and I lean closer.

"Fifty-thousand-dollar robbery leaves police baffled," I read aloud. "This must be it!"

I try to push Lilac out of the chair, so I can read the article but she's not having it.

"I'll read it out loud."

The Hastings police are investigating a bank robbery that happened on Friday evening the 10th of February at the Hastings National Bank in Hastings, Oklahoma. Officers were sent just before 5:30 p.m. to the Hastings National Bank after receiving a call from the bank staff.

Workers told the police the man entered the bank wearing a black hat and red bandana. The suspect walked up to the counter, flourished a gun, and demanded the staff empty the safe.

Police say he was given approximately fifty-thousand dollars before exiting the bank. He fled the scene on foot.

Police believe the suspect is the so-called Black Hat Bandit. The identity of the Black Hat Bandit is currently unknown.

Special agents of the FBI have since also joined the investigation.

"Great Scott!" I throw my arm in the air and whoop. "Mercury was telling the truth. It's an adventure!"

"Hold on. We don't know the Black Hat Bandit is the man to whom Patricia wrote the letter." Lilac had to rain on my parade, didn't she?

"It has to be."

Lilac frowns at me. "Why?"

"One, the letter refers to Robert. And we know the Black Hat Bandit's real name is Robert."

She cocks an eyebrow. "We do?"

"Mercury said so."

She frowns before returning to the microfiche scanner. "Mercury said the Black Hat Bandit was arrested and admitted to the robbery. Did he say when?"

I look at Ellery, and she shrugs. "I guess not," I tell Lilac.

"Why don't the four of you go elsewhere while I do more research?" When no one moves, she continues. "It wasn't a suggestion."

"Fine, we'll be in the main library."

We trudge out of the dark room and make our way to the children's area. I plop down on one of the bean bags and my sisters join me there.

"Good." Juniper rubs her hands. "Now we can return to the topic of Aspen and Lyric."

"There is no Aspen and Lyric."

"You two making out in front of Mom and Dad's house after your date says differently," Ellery points out.

"What did you do? Watch us?"

She rolls her eyes. "Of course not. It was all over the Facebook page within minutes."

My brow wrinkles. "I didn't read anything about Lyric and me on the Facebook page."

"Oops!"

"Oops?" I glare at Ellery. "What do you mean oops?"

"Who cares how she got the news? I want to know why you're fighting a relationship with him. You guys were always hot and heavy in high school. What's changed?" Juniper asks.

"What do you know? You were in grade school when we were in high school."

She waggles her eyebrows. "It's a good thing the Winter Falls School building is for grades from one to twelve then, isn't it?"

"Whatever."

"I don't get you. You have the most eligible bachelor in town after you and you're pushing him away. I wouldn't push him away," Ashlyn claims.

"Yeah, you would, because his name isn't Rowan."

Hurt flashes in her eyes and I regret teasing her. It's not nice when you have a crush on someone for a long ass time and the person doesn't return your feelings. I know. I crushed on Lyric for a decade before he noticed I existed.

"I'm leaving Winter Falls, remember? I can hardly have a relationship with Lyric when he's the Chief of Police and will never leave."

He made his intention to stay in Winter Falls, no matter what, perfectly clear when he refused to even discuss leaving when we graduated college.

"I don't know why you have to return to Dallas. You've done your thing. You've had your adventure. Stay," Ellery implores.

"Besides," Juniper adds, "there's adventure to be had here, too." She points in the rough direction of the microfiche room.

"My whole life is there." I swallow before admitting my biggest fear. "If I start something with Lyric now, I don't know if I'll be able to leave again."

"And never leaving again is a bad thing because?"

I frown at Ashlyn. "I told you. My whole life is in Dallas."

"I hate to say it, big sis, but it's not. Your business and apartment burned down with all your junk in it. What are you returning to?"

"I'm not going to argue with you."

Ashlyn barks out a laugh. "Why not? You usually don't mind."

"Keep it down, West sisters," the librarian yells over at us.

I point to Gratitude who's glaring at us for talking above a whisper despite the library being empty. "There's why."

Small town living is not for me with its nosy neighbors and grapevine that doesn't sleep.

Ellery stands. "Lilac messaged. We may now return."

I roll my eyes before following her back to the microfiche room. When we enter, Lilac hands me a stack of papers.

"What's this?"

"Proof Old Man Mercury isn't a ... I believe the word you would use is a nutcase."

My heart races and my fingers tingle. "What did you find out?"

"The Black Hat Bandit's name was indeed Robert Adams. He confessed to the robbery of the Hastings National Bank when he was arrested in September of 1955 at the scene of another bank robbery in Colorado Springs."

My jaw drops to the floor, and I stare at my younger sister. "We weren't gone but for five minutes."

"Are you doubting my efficiency?"

"Um, no." I wave the copies. "But Old Man Mercury said the Black Hat Bandit was caught robbing a bank in Oklahoma, not Colorado Springs."

Lilac huffs. "First, you doubt my efficiency. Now, you doubt my research."

"No. Sorry. What about Patricia? Did you find anything out about her?"

She frowns. "I don't have anything concrete yet. I read about a fatal train accident in Kansas, but I haven't confirmed Patricia – last name unknown – was a passenger on the train. I've requested copies of newspapers from several Kansas city newspapers as the library doesn't carry them."

"I'm positive Patricia was on the train. The letter said she was." Plus, Old Man Mercury said there was a rumor about her dying in a train crash. It can't be a coincidence.

"In any event, none of this proves the letter was written to Robert Adams or the loot was buried somewhere around Winter Falls."

I don't argue with her. It's enough evidence for me.

"Now what?" I ask.

"Why are you asking me? I'm an environmental engineer, not a treasure hunter. Although, I'm not convinced treasure hunting is an actual profession."

"It is," Juniper says. "I saw it in a movie."

Of course, she did. My little sister loves movies nearly as much as she loves animals, which is saying a lot.

"Does anyone have any ideas?"

I wait but no one has a response.

"Fine. I'll figure it out on my own."

There has to be a book somewhere on how to conduct a treasure hunt. Otherwise, Google is my friend.

Ellery threads her arm through mine. "Not on your own, Aspen. Not in Winter Falls, you aren't, at least."

Too bad Winter Falls isn't my home. A little voice in the back of my mind reminds me it could be, but I shut the voice up as quick as I can. I will return to Dallas. I will rebuild my business. I refuse to be stuck in this small town forever – no matter how much staying for a long visit has reminded me how much I love the place.

Chapter 24

Conspirator – a person who willingly helps another hide information from the entire town to his obvious delight

LYRIC

I smile when Aspen opens her door. "Hello, Sunshine," I greet before kissing her cheek.

Her breath catches, and I duck my head to hide my smirk. Aspen can fight it as much as she wants, but I know she wants me. I plan to use the knowledge to convince her to give us a second chance.

It won't be easy. She thinks distance will keep us apart. She's wrong. I've lived without the woman who holds my heart in her hand for far too long. And now I know she didn't abandon me, there's nothing that can keep me away from her. I don't want to leave my hometown, but if it's the only way I can have Aspen, I'm going to have to consider moving.

"You ready?"

Once a month, the library hosts a movie night since there's no cinema in town. Juniper's in charge of the night, including choosing the movie. And, because it's Juniper, we never know what she'll choose. Aspen's sister has eclectic taste. We've watched everything from Westerns to foreign films with subtitles to the latest spy thriller.

"What's this month's movie choice?" I ask as I grasp Aspen's hand and we begin walking to the library.

"You think Juniper would tell me in advance? She thinks she's a spy protecting the nuclear launch codes when it comes to the monthly movie."

"I don't know how she manages it. Everyone knows everything going on in this town and yet she surprises us each month," I say despite knowing exactly how she manages it.

Aspen stops and turns to study me. I widen my eyes in an attempt to appear innocent, but she doesn't buy it.

"Lyric Journey Alston, you've been helping my sister." She slaps my chest, and I capture her hand.

"It's only a bit of fun. Surprising the old people in this town is not easy."

"Doesn't it bother you how showing a movie this way isn't remotely legal, Mr. Chief of Police?" She adopts a deep voice and mimics. "The unauthorized distribution of this copyrighted work is illegal. Piracy is not a victimless crime."

"Since when do you care about laws?"

She gasps. "You make me sound like a common criminal."

"Oh, babe, there's nothing common about your crimes."

"Crimes?" She sniffs and points her adorable nose in the air. "I've never been convicted of a crime."

"Because no one could ever prove it was you who set the gophers free in the high school." The Great Gopher Outbreak may remain a mystery in town, but I know exactly what happened.

"I have no idea what you're talking about, Chief Alston." She bats her eyelashes. "Besides, I don't think letting wild animals free is a crime."

"Maybe not, but destruction of property is a crime as you well know."

She waves away my comment. "A few holes in school towels in not destruction, especially when those towels were older than most of the pupils."

"Whatever you need to tell yourself to sleep at night, my little criminal."

She rolls her eyes. "What movie have you picked out for us to watch this month?"

"Sorry. It's strictly need to know."

She glares at me for a moment, but after a moment she drops her glare and smirks. "Juniper kept it a secret from you, didn't she?"

I shrug before taking her hand once again and continuing our journey to the library. Juniper has been more secretive than normal about this month's movie. She's obviously up to something, but I'm not bothered since I know all of the West sisters are on my side. I don't know if it's because they want their big sis to move back to Winter Falls or if they want us together. I'm not bothered. Either way, I win.

When we enter the library, Juniper is there to greet us. She shoves a bucket of popcorn into Aspen's arms. "Extra butter the way my big sis loves it," she says before handing me a pail of ice filled with beer. "Today's word is y'all."

Aspen wrinkles her nose at the six beers in the pail. "I don't remember there being alcoholic drinks at movie night when we were kids."

"This is adult movie night."

I point to an empty loveseat. It's empty because Juniper and her sisters made certain no one sat here. The 'reserved for the Chief' sign I saw Ashlyn yank away when we entered kind of gave them away.

The 'loveseat' is barely large enough for two 'normal' people. Since I'm six-foot-three with broad shoulders to match my height, it's going to be a tight squeeze. I love the West sisters right now.

"Adult Winter Falls is way different than I remember it," Aspen says as she settles in and looks around at everyone eating and drinking and generally having a good time.

"But it's fun, isn't it?" I decide to push it. "Probably way more fun than Dallas."

She ignores my comment and grabs a beer from our pail. "Do I need to worry about Juniper having a drinking problem?"

"Your sister works her butt off at the wild animal refuge six days a week. She deserves to let loose once in a while."

Aspen frowns. "She works too hard. Don't they have any other staff to help out?"

"I don't think Juniper trusts anyone with *her* animals."

"I'm surprised she doesn't sleep in the barn with them."

The lights flicker before Juniper walks to the front of the room.

"Welcome to Winter Falls movie night!" Everyone claps and hoots and hollers until she shushes them.

"Tonight's movie is ..." She pauses before staring straight into Aspen's eyes and announcing, "*Sweet Home Alabama.*"

Aspen springs to her feet. "Nope. No way. She did this on purpose."

I grasp her hand and yank her back down. "Of course, she did. I'm relieved the movie choice is this tame."

"Tame! She picked a movie about a woman who made it in the big city but has to return to her small hometown to ask for a divorce from her first love. Needless to say, she never stopped loving him and they end up together in the end. She's comparing me and my situation to Melanie Carmichael."

"You think?" I chuckle. "Your sister never was much for subtlety."

She smacks me with her beer. "You're not helping."

"You should feel lucky she didn't choose *Basic Instinct* or *9½ Weeks.*"

She gasps. "She wouldn't."

"Sunshine, there's a reason this is adult movie night. You wouldn't believe some of the foreign films she picked out. Europeans do not have a problem with nudity in films."

"Since when do you have a problem with nudity in films?"

I dip my mouth to her ear and growl, "Since I have to sit next to a woman I want to strip naked in a room with a bunch of other people who won't fail to notice or comment."

She shivers, and I grasp the opportunity to nip her earlobe.

"If the Chief of Police would quiet down now, we're ready to begin the film," Ashlyn yells.

I sigh before leaning back and throwing my arm over Aspen's shoulder to draw her near. She tries to shove me away. "Calm down, Sunshine. We have popcorn and beer and the lights are dim. Let's enjoy ourselves."

She elbows me. "Don't tell me to calm down." She narrows her eyes on me. "And if you try to cop a feel, copper, I'm twisting your nipples off."

"I'd let him cop a feel," Petal hollers from behind us.

"Woman, behave," her husband, Orion, growls.

The lights switch off, and the movie begins. Aspen is stiff in my arms at first, but after a few minutes, she settles. I breathe in the smell of her shampoo. Wild cherry. It's the same scent it's always been. I can't smell wild cherries without feeling a buzz of excitement in my veins.

Thirty minutes into the film, Aspen grunts as she places her empty beer in our pail. "I'm going to be wasted if they don't stop saying y'all."

"Good. My evil plan is working."

"I think you mean my evil plan, Chief," Juniper says from somewhere behind us.

Aspen tucks her legs under her butt and cuddles into me. Whoever's plan it is, it's definitely working. Five minutes later, Aspen snores. Damn. Maybe this plan isn't working after all.

When the movie ends and the lights switch on, Aspen startles awake.

"I fell asleep."

I maneuver her until she's straddling my lap. "Now you'll never know if they found true love."

She snorts. "It's a romance. Of course, they found true love. It's a requisite to being a romance."

I tuck one of her curls behind her ear. "You always were a book nerd."

"Duh. I opened a bookstore."

My stomach clenches at the reminder of her life outside of Winter Falls. I ignore it and notice Aspen's eyes are trained on my mouth. I take the look for the obvious invitation it is and meld my lips to hers. She moans and I shove my tongue past her lips to explore her mouth.

"Ahem." I hear someone clearing their voice behind me, but I ignore them. Nothing could possibly be more important than what I'm doing right now.

"Excuse me!" The voice is louder this time, but I continue to ignore them. Why would I pay them any attention when my lips are touching the softest lips in the world and my tongue is dueling with Aspen's?

Splash! A bucket of ice water rains down upon us. Aspen squeals.

"What the hell?" I growl up at Juniper.

She smiles. "I need to close up for the night."

"You couldn't give me the keys to close up like you've done dozens of times before?"

"Nope."

"Is it illegal to kill your sister?" Aspen growls as she glares up at Juniper.

"No jury would convict you in this instance," I tell her before lifting her off of my lap to stand.

Juniper squeals and throws the keys in our direction. "Don't forget to switch the lights off," she orders as she runs off.

"Do you want a sister? I know one you can have for free," Aspen mutters.

"Come on. I'll escort you home."

This is not how I intended our evening to end, but I had Aspen cuddled in my arms for hours. It's progress. Slow progress. But slow progress is better than no progress.

Chapter 25

Busybody – a meddling woman who has no shame at all in her meddling

THE BELL ABOVE THE door at the bookstore rings, and I glance over at the entrance to find Saffron walking inside. When she uses her walker to prop the door open, I rush to her aid.

"Child, I've got this."

I raise my hands and step back to let her enter under her own steam.

"You're looking good, Saffron."

She surveys the bookstore. "I tell you what's looking good. *Fall Into a Good Book* has never looked this good."

I feel my cheeks heat. "Thank you. It's actually been a lot of fun."

I sound surprised. I think I am surprised. I forgot how much fun it is to play around with a business and discover ways to make it succeed.

"Show me the tourist corner the entire town is buzzing about."

"I don't know about the entire town," I mumble as I lead her to the corner where I've made a display of local products as well as put out pamphlets of local tourist attractions.

"How are the sales thus far?"

This could take a while and she doesn't look too steady on her feet.

"Shall we sit?"

We settle into one of the many reading areas laced throughout the store, and I open my tablet to talk numbers. This is my least favorite part of owning a business, but important nonetheless – if you want to make money. And money is, unfortunately, necessary to pay the bills. Stupid bills.

"And," I continue after going over the sales from the tourist corner. "The book club was a big success as well. I'm hoping to add an open mic night considering how well the book club went. And, if it goes well, we can always try other activity nights. Paint and Sip is very popular in Dallas. And there's always author book signings."

"Author book signings!" A customer who was browsing the stacks behind us shouts. "Who's coming? Please say it's J.R.R. Tolkien. Those *Lord of the Rings* movies are the best."

"Tolkien died in 1973."

Her eyes widen. "You're having a séance? I heard this town was full of hippies, but I didn't realize you did séances at the bookstore. I'll have to tell all my friends."

"Wait. We don't—" She bustles out of the store before I can tell her we definitely don't do séances in this store.

Saffron pats my knee. "Don't worry. If she comes back, you can ask Cayenne to help out."

"Cayenne? She's a yoga instructor. How can she help?"

"Trust me. She can help."

"Wait. You said *I* can ask Cayenne. What about you? When are you coming back to work?"

Before she can answer, another customer arrives. I stand to ask if she needs any help. "Are you in search of a particular book or do you want to browse?"

"I'm searching for a particular book. When is C.S. Lewis going to come out with another *Chronicles of Narnia* book?"

"Have you read all seven books?"

"Seven books? But there were only three films."

Great. Two customers in one hour who think film adaptations are better than the book. Spoiler alert – the book is *always* better.

"Shall I show you to the children's section?" I motion toward the back of the store.

"No thanks," she grunts before leaving.

I sigh as I sit back down across from Saffron. "You should probably add a movie section."

"Not I, darling. You."

My forehead wrinkles as I stare at her. This is the second time she said *I* had to make changes. "What are you talking about?"

"I want to sell you my store."

My eyes widen and my mouth falls open. "I... I ... I..." I can't form a coherent sentence. I finally decide on, "I don't know what to say."

"I know you'll need time to think about it, but I thought we should talk numbers now anyway. If you don't know how much I'm asking, you can't properly consider the offer."

"But I'm not staying in Winter Falls."

She cocks an eyebrow. "You were canoodling with Chief Alston at movie night the other night."

"I didn't read anything about Lyric and me on the Facebook group. Is there another group page I'm not a member of?"

She grins. "Half the town was at movie night. There was no need to post on the Facebook page. Although, the picture Ashlyn sent me of Juniper dousing the two of you with water would have been a big hit."

I bury my face in my hands. Of course, Ashlyn took a picture. She'll probably have it framed and gift it to me for Christmas.

I clear my throat. "Whatever is going on with Lyric and me is of no consequence."

"It isn't?" Sage asks, and I startle so hard I nearly fall out of my chair. Where did she come from? "Because Lyric has been strutting around like a lion who took down some poor gazelle all week."

"Am I the gazelle in this analogy? I'm not prey just because I was the slowest runner in the history of the Winter Falls cross-country team." It's true. I have a plaque and everything.

"Which is probably why you got taken down."

I close my eyes and count to ten before I lose my mind and do something incredibly stupid like kick her out of the bookstore. She wouldn't leave, but she'd create enough of a ruckus to cause every single person on Main Street to come over and find out what's going on. The last thing I need right now is more peeping Toms in my life.

"What's going on?" Petal asks. "Did Saffron offer Aspen the store yet? What did she say?"

"Hush, Petal. We're still discussing Lyric and Aspen," Feather adds.

I study the book stacks around me. Is there a secret entrance I don't know about? How cool would that be? Except for when these nosy, intrusive women show up without an invitation.

"Have you been hiding in the store? I didn't hear the bell go off."

Feather points to the rear of the store. "The back door isn't locked."

No secret entrance then. Bummer. I add 'lock the back door to keep nosy busybodies out of the store' to my daily to-do list.

Saffron frowns at her friends. "I told you to give me some time to convince her."

I should have known they planned to ambush me.

"You were taking too long," Feather says.

"And we want to hear if Lyric took Aspen home and rocked her world."

I eye the backdoor. I'm not a coward if I sneak out, am I?

The bell above the front door rings, and I leap from my chair at the chance of a distraction. "Sorry, ladies. Duty calls."

I practically tackle the customer. "How may I help you today?"

"I'm searching for that new release. I can't remember the name, but the cover is blue."

"Do you know what the book is about?"

"It's supposed to be a great read."

Very helpful. Not.

"What's the genre of the book?"

"Genre?"

"Romance? Mystery? Thriller? Any of these ring a bell?"

"Here." Sage shoves the latest book in the *Outlander* series at me.

I refuse to touch the book. "This book is not a standalone, you have to read the series in order."

Sage rolls her eyes at me before asking the customer. "Have you watched the *Outlander* series on television?'

"Who hasn't?" She sighs. "Sam Heughan is positively dreamy."

Sage nudges me out of the way and hands the woman the book. "You'll love this."

"Thank you." The woman gives her some money before leaving the store.

"Another happy customer," Sage declares. I glare at her as I snatch the money out of her hand and stomp to the cash register. "I can't believe you," I complain while I enter the transaction. "You know a television series can't compare to the book."

"I don't know. *The Handmaid's Tale* was pretty accurate."

I throw my arms in the air. "I give up."

"I'm afraid I'm going to have to agree with Aspen this time. You busybodies need to leave us alone so we can discuss business." Hallelujah. At least Saffron is talking sense.

"I can't believe you called me a busybody. It's not my fault I know everything going on in town since I work as the police dispatcher. This is job discrimination," Sage complains. Petal and Feather nod in agreement.

I collapse in the chair across from Saffron. "What's the big deal with leaving? Saffron's going to tell you everything we discuss here anyway."

"She won't pry into your relationship with Lyric the way we can," Feather explains.

"There's nothing to pry into. Lyric and I don't have a relationship."

Two dates and a bit of making out isn't a relationship, is it? Even if the man you're making out with was your first love? And his kisses make your toes curl and tingles explode throughout your body? This is why I can't get involved with Lyric. The entire scenario has complicated written all over it in big, fat capital letters and backlit by neon lights.

"Still in denial then. I'll inform the troops," Sage says as she herds Petal and Feather out of the store.

"I'm not in denial," I yell after her.

"The thing about denial is, you don't realize you're in it until you're done with it," she yells back.

"Now," Saffron says when the door shuts behind them, "let's discuss my offer in detail."

"I'm telling you, I'm not staying in Winter Falls." My words don't sound as forceful as I want them to. I want them to? Do I want them to sound forceful? Am I doubting leaving?

Damn Lyric! A few kisses and my conviction to return home is wavering.

"In case you change your mind, I'd prefer if you heard me out."

I motion for her to continue. "Of course."

When I escort Saffron out of the bookstore thirty minutes later, I have to consciously tell my mouth to stop gapping open. Why did I ever think Saffron was the sane one of the busybodies?

She's lost it if she's offering to sell the store to me for the price she quoted today. Her asking price doesn't begin to cover the cost of the real estate, let alone the value of the business and its inventory. But no matter how many times I told her she was forgetting to add a zero to the price, she stuck to her guns.

As I watch Saffron make her way down the sidewalk of Main Street, I can't help but wonder how it would feel if I could say yes to her offer. I shake my head. What am I thinking? Of course, I could say yes if I wanted to. But I don't want to. My life is in Dallas.

My business, my apartment – they're all in Dallas. *What about your friends and family?* An obnoxious voice in my head asks. Too bad for Ms. Obnoxious I'm ignoring her. *And Lyric?* Ms. Obnoxious obviously didn't get the memo on me ignoring her.

Chapter 26

Surprise – when someone calls out of the blue and offers you everything you want except you don't want it anymore. You think. Maybe. Ah, hell, who knows?

I finish closing out the register for the day and stuff the money in a deposit bag before locking up the bookstore. Since Saffron left, I've been walking around in a daze. She wasn't joking about offering to sell me the store. Not with the detailed spreadsheets she showed me. Based on her accounting software, I didn't think she knew what a spreadsheet was let alone how to use one. How wrong I was!

But I can't return home. There's a reason Thomas Wolfe's final book was titled *You Can't Go Home Again* after all. Of course, I didn't pull an asshole move and write a book about Winter Falls and portray the residents in an unfavorable way either.

As I make my way down Main Street, everyone smiles and waves at me. Lennon asks me if I'm coming to the baseball game tomorrow night, and Cayenne reminds me of the hot yoga class this weekend.

Okay, fine. I'll admit it. I miss Winter Falls. It's reassuring when everyone knows your name. It can be awkward when everyone knows every detail of your life, but it's also heartwarming when they know your home burned down and stop by your parent's house with clothes for you.

Peace falls in line beside me. "Aspen."

"What's up, Peace?"

"We like to accompany the business owners to the bank when they do their daily deposit."

In Winter Falls? Where crime is practically non-existent? I'm not buying.

"What are you really doing?"

He shrugs. "Word on the street—"

"I think you mean Sage, the queen of the busybodies."

He smiles. "Correction. Sage told everyone within hearing distance today about Saffron's offer. Lyric wanted to come check on you, but he's worried you'll think he's pressuring you."

"He told you that?"

I have a hard time believing Chief Alston would confess anything to his officers about his love life especially since he knows I'll hear about it and have to enact revenge. Lyric with a shaved head is not attractive. As everyone in town knows from the time when he thought me saying I'm fine actually meant I'm fine. He won't make that mistake ever again.

"Well, no. But he was thinking it."

"You a mind reader now, Peace?"

He shrugs and we continue on in silence. I throw the deposit bag into the drop box.

"I now absolve you of your duties," I announce in a fake British accent once the box clicks shut.

"You're not going to give me even a tiny hint which way you're leaning?"

I shove him away. "Being nosy isn't attractive."

He waggles his eyebrows. "And yet women can't resist me." He whistles as he saunters off.

My phone rings and I dig it out of my bag. The display indicates the insurance company is calling. Hallelujah!

"This is Aspen West."

I listen for the next minutes as my insurance company explains in more detail than I can honestly understand how they have now finished their investigation into the fire and my insurance claim with regard to my building.

"And what does this mean for me?" I ask when the woman pauses to take a breath.

"It means we'll be processing a check for the amount of your claim."

"Thank you," I squeal before I hang up.

Yes! Finally! The insurance company is paying me the money they owe me, and I can return home to Dallas. But wait. What about the bookstore? What about Saffron's offer? Dang it all to hell. I knew getting involved with Lyric would cause me no end of troubles. And, yes, this is all Lyric's fault.

"Why me?" I scream. I hear several doors open up and people step into the street at the commotion I caused.

Great. Now everyone's going to think I'm having a breakdown. They should seriously pay me for the entertainment I provide this town. I smile and wave at everyone as if I'm not a complete lunatic. As soon as everyone returns to whatever they were doing, I duck into an alleyway and make my way out of town to the trail to the waterfall.

I hike through the woods until I come to the top of the falls. I find my favorite boulder to sit on and collapse.

I know I've been saying I'll return to Dallas as soon as my insurance money comes, but I figured I had more time in town. More time with Lyric to be exact. Groan. I knew I shouldn't have started anything with the man. The sexy Chief of Police turns my mind to mush and not the good kind with cinnamon and brown sugar either.

Mom sits down next to me. I don't jump in surprise. An armadillo would have heard her clomping through the woods, and armadillos are completely deaf.

"How'd you find me?"

She smirks. "I think half of the town saw you shout *Why me?* to the sky before you stomped your way to the trail to the river."

"I miss the privacy of the big city."

She cocks an eyebrow. "Do you?"

I shrug. "Sometimes this town is too much."

She indicates the waterfall and river with a sweep of her arm. "But look where you are now? There's no place to compare with this in Dallas."

"What about culture?" Do I sound as desperate as I feel to prove to her how Dallas is my home now?

"What about the open mic night?"

"What? How do you know about it already?" It's merely an idea at this point. "Is there some messenger group to spread gossip in this town I'm not aware of?"

Mom glances toward the water and starts humming.

"You are shitting me! There is! Why am I not in the group?"

"Residents only."

"Whatever," I mutter and stare out onto the water once again.

Mom isn't one to let me sit in silence, though. "What's going on? Are you not happy with the offer Saffron made?"

I don't bother asking her how she knows about Saffron's offer. She probably knew Saffron was going to offer to sell me her business before I did. Not to mention Mrs. Blabbermouth, aka Sage, probably told the whole town by now.

"It's a ridiculous offer."

She pats my thigh. "I'm sure there's room to negotiate. Your dad and I discussed it, and we're willing to help with the down payment."

My nose scrunches. "You are?" They didn't give me a dime to help me set up my business in Dallas.

"It's only fair since we helped Ellery buy the mansion to establish *The Inn on Main*."

They did? Ellery didn't tell me. Huh. Maybe people in this town can keep a secret after all.

"It doesn't matter. I'm not staying." I might as well go ahead and tell her the insurance company called. She probably knows already anyway. "The insurance company called. They're cutting me a check."

"Good, baby girl. You deserve the money."

"Thanks."

"But you don't have to use the insurance money to rebuild in Dallas. You can use the money to buy *Fall Into a Good Book*. Saffron is impressed with the changes you've made."

Here we go again. I knew she wouldn't let this go.

I try to force some enthusiasm in my voice. "I want to return to Dallas."

"You do? Why?"

"It's my home."

"You've had your adventure. There's no reason for you to return to Dallas."

I rear back. "My adventure? You think moving to Texas and setting up a business in a town where I knew no one was for an adventure?"

She stares at me in the way all mothers have. You know what I mean. Like she can read every thought in my mind and says, "It wasn't?"

I can't hold her gaze. Not when we both know she's right. Not completely right, but maybe my impetus for leaving Winter Falls had a bit to do with wanting to experience an adventure.

"But I built a life there."

"You have? Where are all your friends? Where were they when you had to sell your jewelry to pay for that hideous car to drive home in?"

I grit my teeth. "You weren't supposed to find out." I didn't want her or anyone else knowing how desperate I was when I arrived back home last month.

"My statement stands. What kind of life do you have in Dallas if you don't have good friends there?"

"I haven't had a whole lot of time to build friendships. I've been working seven days a week on growing my business."

"Another reason to stay here. You don't need to work seven days a week here."

What she means is, I can't work seven days a week in Winter Falls. The founders of the town were determined to not get caught in the 'capitalism trap' and passed a law requiring all businesses to be closed at least one day a week.

"I don't mind working hard."

She bumps my shoulder. "I know, but you don't have to."

We sit in silence for a while as we stare into the water of the falls. Watching the river bubble over the rocks is soothing in a way I haven't found anywhere else in the world. Staring out at the Trinity River in Dallas certainly doesn't bring me this kind of peace, especially not with the city skyline in the background.

"There are adventures to be found in Winter Falls, too. Perhaps a treasure hunt?"

Good grief. Is nothing kept private in this town? I can't even count on my sisters to keep their mouths shut. So much for the whole town not sticking their noses in our treasure hunt.

"Which sister told you?"

"None. Gratitude messaged me."

I should have known. The librarian has held a grudge against me since the time I accidentally pushed one of the bookshelves over. It wasn't my fault. I assumed the shelving was bolted to the ground when I started to climb the shelf. Had it been, I totally would have won the bet.

We fall into silence again. This time she clears her throat before she speaks.

"And what about Lyric? That boy is as crazy about you today as he was when you were teenagers and sneaking off to fool around in the treehouse."

I groan. "Can't you pretend you didn't know about the treehouse?"

"Nope." She smirks. "If I didn't know about your romantic rendezvous, I never would have asked your father to install a wood-burning stove in there. Would you have rather frozen to death?"

"Maybe," I mumble.

"Don't be such a prude. I heard you two in there more than once. Would you have preferred I said something then?"

"NO!" She heard Lyric and me having sex? Talk about embarrassing.

Mom bumps my shoulder. "And I know you're as crazy about Lyric as you were when you were ten. You followed him around with hearts in your eyes for years."

I bury my face in my hands. "Thanks for the reminder of how pathetic I was."

"It's not pathetic considering Lyric fell in love with you."

"Can we stop brandishing the L-word around?"

"Sure." She shrugs. "Have you and Lyric reacquainted yourselves in a carnal way?"

I spring to my feet. "I am now declaring this heart-to-heart finished."

"Of course, you are. You always were such a prude when it came to talking about sex. Now, the actual act of sex? You weren't such a prude then."

I start speed walking back to the house. "I'm not discussing my sex life with you."

Mom isn't letting me go without a parting shot. "Tell me you'll give Lyric a chance and I'll stop talking," she shouts after me.

I stop and spin around to confront her. "You're blackmailing me?"

She rolls her eyes. "How else am I ever going to become a grandmother?"

I throw my arms into the air. "And now you want me to have Lyric's children! You are wackadoodle."

I don't wait for her reply. I can't listen to any more of this. First, she's trying to convince me to stay in town, and then she's pressuring me to get pregnant. Pregnant? Yikes! Except there's no spike of fear to accompany my internal thoughts. Being pregnant doesn't scare me? Now, there's a terrifying thought.

Chapter 27

Catch – a word sounding suspiciously similar to fetch

"Hey, Sunshine." Lyric leans over the check-out counter to kiss my cheek. "Are you ready to go?"

"Ready to go? It's not—" I glance at the time on my watch. What? It's already six? Where did the day go?

"A bit preoccupied today?" I shrug. "Saffron offering you the store threw you for a curve, didn't it?"

Sigh. I knew this was coming. The big push. I expected Lyric to show up at my parent's house last night and start pressuring away. To his credit, he waited a whole day.

"I'm not going to pressure you to stay in Winter Falls."

"You're not. Who are you and what have you done with Lyric Journey Alston?"

He tweaks my nose. "Smart ass."

"I'm not a smart ass. You know you want me to stay in town and Saffron's offer is the perfect excuse."

"I'm not going to deny wanting you to stay. I never wanted you to leave in the first place. But I know better than to trap a butterfly."

"I'm a butterfly now, am I?" I flap my arms like they're wings.

Lyric chuckles before setting some letters on the counter. "Come on, let's go. Softball waits for no man, including the Chief of Police."

"Hold on. What's this?"

"Your mail. Petal gave it to me. I guess it was delivered to *Sensual Scents* instead of here."

I sift through the envelopes to check if there's anything urgent I need to deal with immediately. I pause when I notice a larger envelope. What's this? I flip it over to read the return address. The Junction City Library.

"Yes!" I shout before ripping open the envelope to discover it filled with several newspaper clippings. Waffles lifts his lazy head and gives off a half-hearted bark. "Oh, shush you. This is exciting."

"What is it?"

I don't answer Lyric's question as I'm too busy rifling through the clippings. I notice a headline 'Rail Wreck Fatal to 50'. This must be it! I skim through the article.

Rail Wreck Fatal to 50

The toll of dead and missing in Tuesday's Junction City train crash mounted to fifty as railway officials pieced together the story of Kansas's worst railway disaster.

The train was traveling through Kansas on Tuesday evening when the Rock Island Train that runs between Chicago and Denver derailed west of Junction City, toppling several cars onto their sides, authorities said.

The westbound Rock Island Train derailed at about 4 pm near Junction City. Geary County sheriff's dispatcher said at least fifty people died. She did not have more details.

The cause of the accident was not immediately clear and federal safety authorities will investigate.

"Please tell me there's a list of passengers," I pray as I flip through the newspaper clippings.

"Aha!" I cry when I find another clipping with the passenger list. "Patricia, Patricia, Patricia." I run my finger down the list of the names checking for anyone with the first name of Patricia since I don't know her last name.

My finger stops on the name Patricia Hall. "She's real. The Black Hat Bandit's lover is real."

I wave the clipping at Lyric. "Look! It's true. Old Man Mercury wasn't lying. There's gold in them thar hills. Well, not gold. Cash. Fifty-thousand buckaroos, in fact."

Waffles barks. "Yes, Waffles, there's money enough to buy you lots of treats and toys." He gives off a mini howl, obviously satisfied with my answer, before laying back down once more.

"What are you talking about?" Lyric asks.

Whoa. He doesn't know? The gossip gang hasn't kept up with our treasure hunt? The librarian, Gratitude, hasn't spilled the news to the entire town? Awesome! I scan the bookstore to make sure it's empty before locking the front door.

"You remember the letter I found in the storage room?" He nods. "I talked to Old Man Mercury, and he told us about a bank robber who's rumored to have hidden fifty-thousand dollars somewhere near Winter Falls before it was Winter Falls."

Lyric crosses his arms over his chest, and I'm momentarily distracted by the sight of his bulging biceps. Since when are biceps sexy? Since right now apparently.

"Ahem." He clears his throat, and I force my gaze away from his biceps to find him smirking at me. My face heats, but I ignore it. He doesn't need to know how sexy I find him. Oh, who am I kidding? He knows exactly how sexy I think he is.

"And now you're on a wild goose chase to find the money."

"Wild goose chase? I think you mean treasure hunt."

He chuckles. "You and your adventures."

I pause at the word adventures. He's the second person in two days to remark upon my need for an adventure. Is it true? Did I leave Winter Falls because I wanted an adventure I couldn't find here? I shove those thoughts away. I'll contemplate them later. Much, much later.

"If you're going to make fun, I won't share my loot with you."

He steps closer and places his hands on my hips. "I don't need your loot, Sunshine. I just need you."

Before I have a chance to remind him we're not in a relationship, his lips meet mine and any coherent thoughts fly straight out of my head. I moan as his tongue invades my mouth. He pulls me flush to his body and when I feel his hard length press against me, my nipples harden, and my belly dips. *Yes.*

Bang! Bang! Bang!

Lyric wrests his lips from mine and growls at the intrusion. My sister Ashlyn waves at us from the sidewalk in front of the store.

"See you at the game!" She shouts before skipping off.

"She banged on the window on purpose," he grumbles.

I soothe my hand down his chest. "Of course, she did. You have met my sister before, haven't you?"

He sighs before grasping my hand. "Come on. We better go before she tells the entire town we were having sex in the store."

I bump his hip. "As if you'd care."

"I wouldn't, but you would, and it's my job to protect you."

"The big bad Chief of Police is going to protect me." I flutter my eyelashes at him.

He rolls his eyes. "Waffles. Come!"

My dog that barely listens to me on the best of days jumps to follow his order. I frown. Waffles is supposed to be on my side. I glare at him, but when he gazes up at me with those big, brown eyes and his doggy smile, my anger drifts away. He's too darn cute to be mad at.

"I'm surprised you don't play in the softball league. You were Mr. Jock Of All Sports back in school."

He shrugs. "With my job, I can't always make the games."

"Ah, yes. The woes of being the big enchilada of the police department in the great city of Winter Falls."

He ruffles my hair. "You'd be surprised by the stuff that happens here."

Now, I'm interested. "Examples. I need examples."

"I could tell you, but then I'd have to kill you."

For teasing me, I stick my tongue out at him.

We reach the park with the baseball field, and Ellery waves us over. Lyric goes off to get us some refreshments while I join her.

"The game's nearly finished. I'm surprised you made it. Rumor has it you were knocking boots in front of the big window at the bookstore for all to see."

I groan. "Ashlyn is a big, fat liar."

She points at my face. "Made you blush!"

"I guess I won't tell you about the letter I got today then."

She narrows her eyes on me. "What letter?"

"From the Junction City library."

She claps her hands. "You'll have to tell me later when the Chief of Police isn't giving me the stink eye for stealing you away from him." She points to Lyric.

I glance over my shoulder to find him strutting our way. His jeans are molded to those strong thigh muscles I may be slightly obsessed with and his biceps bulge as he carries a tray of drinks and food.

Ellery leans close to whisper, "You're drooling."

I ignore her. I am not drooling.

Lyric picks up one of the hotdogs from the tray and throws it at Waffles who catches it in the air before inhaling the treat. Ah, so this is why my dog prefers him over me.

"Stop spoiling him. He's going to get fat," I complain.

Lyric hands me a beer. "Don't be jealous. I bought you a hotdog, too."

"A hotdog is hardly a meal." My words don't stop me from stuffing the hotdog into my mouth.

"Which is why I thought you could come back to my house after the game's finished for dinner. I'll put some steaks on the grill."

I should stop this right here. Dinner at Lyric's house spells relationship. But apparently the level-headed business owner I am when I'm in Dallas has taken a hike in preference to the devil-may-care girl I am when I'm in Winter Falls.

I bump his shoulder. "Why, Chief, are you asking me out?"

His eyes flare. "I do know how much you enjoy steak."

Ellery feigns gagging next to me. "You two are gross."

"What are you? Twelve? Who says the word gross anymore?"

"I do," Juniper says as she plops down on the ground next to Waffles. He immediately rolls on his back for belly rubs. My dog is an attention whore.

"Here's an example of when you've had a truly 'gross' day. When a dog decides to eat the poop of a cat and then throws it up all over the goat enclosure where the goats proceed to eat it."

Ellery's not faking her gags now. "Stop. I choose dirty toilets over your job any day."

I shiver. "As long as the poop is actually in the toilet." Blech. I have nightmares of the day I helped her clean at the inn.

"Maybe we should pay attention to the game," Lilac says as she sits down next to Ellery.

"Is she serious?" Ellery whispers to me.

"Why else are we here if not to watch the game?"

I hold up my beer. "To drink." I hold up my hotdog wrapper. "And eat."

"Are you aware of the ingredients in a hot dog?"

I put my hand up in a stop gesture. "I don't want to know."

Lyric wraps his arm around my shoulder. "Never a dull day when the West sisters are around."

I ignore his comment and how safe and secure his arm is making me feel and turn my attention to the game. It's the bottom of the seventh, and the home team is losing by seven runs. We've already got two outs, but there's one more batter left.

"Come on, Bat Intentions. You got this," I shout.

Petal's husband, Orion, winks at me as he struts to home plate. He does a few practice swings before stepping up to bat. The pitcher serves him a slow ball and *bam!* Orion hits the ball with a whack! The crowd jumps to its feet.

"Run! Run! Run!" I scream along with everyone else.

The third baseman yells at the outfielder. "Catch the ball! Catch it!"

Waffles ears lift when he hears the word catch. He springs to his feet with a whoof and he's off like a rocket after the ball.

"No, Waffles!" I wail, but he doesn't hear me or – the more likely scenario – he doesn't pay any attention to me.

Lyric hands me his beer. "I got this," he says before sprinting after my dog at full speed.

Waffles bounds across the baseball field, past the shortstop who throws his mitt at him but misses, straight toward the left fielder who doesn't notice the dog as his eyes are trained on the ball. The outfielder raises his mitt to catch the ball, but just as the ball reaches him, Waffles tackles him to the ground.

Lyric is right on Waffles' tail and yanks my dog off the player by his collar. As soon as the player is liberated, he lifts his mitt into the air – the mitt which still contains the ball.

"You're out!" the ump declares.

Everyone from Winter Falls groans. It's official. We've lost.

I collect our trash as Lyric strolls across the field with Waffles barking and running circles around him.

Lyric smiles as he joins me. "Come on. Let's get you some real food."

He doesn't wait for my response before leading me away, Waffles following behind us like he's a trained animal and not the mutt that just tackled one of the opposing team's outfielders.

Chapter 28

Good idea and bad idea – can be incredibly difficult to tell the two apart

LYRIC

I smile when Aspen gasps upon entering my house. I'm happy she likes it since I'm going to do my utmost to make my house her home no matter how long it takes.

"What do you think, Waffles? Are you going to slip and slide all over these wooden floors?"

At her words, the dog rushes off toward the kitchen. He flies past the entrance and ends up on his furry bottom before scrambling with his paws to spin around and finally enter the kitchen.

"Slip and slide it is."

"What do you think of the house?"

Aspen beams. "I think I can't believe how gorgeous the place is. I love this staircase." She caresses the handrail I spent an entire month of weekends stripping and sanding before staining it dark walnut to contrast with the white of the balusters and risers.

"And these French doors leading into the living room. Did you add them?"

"I considered removing all the walls and making the first floor open plan, but when the contractor quoted me the cost, I decided open plan isn't all it's cracked up to be." As soon as I managed to get my heart beating again.

She laughs before opening the French doors and entering the living room. Against the opposite wall is a stone fireplace while the wall facing the street features a large picture window with a window seat in the alcove.

She settles on the window seat. "I could sit here for hours and read," she says while her hand strokes the cushion.

I know. It's why I added the window seat.

She cocks her head. "What am I hearing?" She stands. "Oh no. Waffles!"

She rushes through the archway to the kitchen to find her dog eating from his bowl. "Why do you have doggy bowls? You don't have a dog."

"I wanted Waffles to feel welcome here should he ever visit me."

Her eyes narrow. "Awful presumptuous of you."

I lean against the kitchen counter and cross my arms over my chest. I note how her eyes dip to my arms and heat. Considering her reaction to my clothed arms, I can't wait to experience her reaction to my naked body. My cock twitches at the idea.

"Your dog does love me."

She rolls her eyes. "He's usually frightened of strangers, but he seems to love everyone in Winter Falls."

I'm tempted to tell her *because this is where he belongs,* but I keep my mouth shut. She already thinks I'm pushing her too much to settle here. Subtly is the name of the game.

"It is a pretty cool town," I say, and she sighs. I guess I need to work on my subtly.

Waffles finishes his food and nudges Aspen. "What do you want, baby boy?" He nudges her forward again until she's practically in my arms. I knew there was a reason I loved this dog.

I wrap my arms around Aspen and bring her close. "I think your dog wants us to cuddle."

She glares down at him. "Did your grandmother put you up to this?"

He woofs before rushing off to explore the rest of my house.

Aspen presses against my shoulders. "I should go make sure he doesn't destroy your house."

I tighten my arms to keep her right where she is. "He's fine. He won't destroy anything." I lean forward to whisper in her ear. "Besides, we have better things to do."

"We do?" she asks but tilts her head to give me better access to her neck.

I bite her earlobe before licking a path from her ear down her neck to the junction with her shoulder. She shivers in my arms.

"We most certainly do," I tell her before I nudge the fabric of her shirt aside with my nose and begin planting kisses along her shoulder.

Her hands grasp my hips and squeeze. Some things never change. She still enjoys my lips on the naked skin of her shoulders. Time to use my knowledge for the greater good.

I rub my nose against her skin before moving on to her other shoulder. I give thanks for her loose top when I nudge it to the side and the entire thing falls down her arms to reveal her white, lace bra.

Her breasts strain against the lace as she pants for breath. I lightly trace the outer edge of the material with my finger, and she moans and arches her back to shove her chest into my hands. It's an invitation I will never refuse.

I drag her bra cups down until her breasts are revealed in all their glory. They're round and plump and all mine. I waste no time dipping my head to draw one of her nipples into my mouth.

"Lyric!" Her fingers thread through my hair, and she uses the hold to keep me right where she wants me. You won't hear me complain.

While one hand kneads and tweaks her breast, my mouth bites and sucks on her other one until she's rocking against me.

I lift my head and she mewls. "I think we should move this to my bedroom."

She looks around as if suddenly realizing we're in my kitchen with windows where anyone passing by my backyard can peer in and catch us in the act. "I don't think this is a good idea."

I freeze. "I think it's a fantastic idea, but if you're not sure, we'll stop." *Please don't want to stop.* My cock throbs in my pants.

"I didn't say I wanted to stop. I said this wasn't a good idea. Not the same thing."

"Alrighty then." I lift her and throw her over my shoulder.

She slaps my back. "I can walk. You don't have to give me a ride to your bedroom."

"Sunshine, I'm going to give you a ride, all right."

She snorts. "Corny."

I dash up the stairs with her bobbing up and down on my shoulder. As soon as we're in my bedroom, I throw her on my bed. She giggles as she bounces. I kneel on the bed and crawl up her length until my body is covering hers.

"I'll show you corny."

"Promises. Promises."

I thrust my cock into her unfortunately clothed center. "How's this for fulfilling a promise?"

She arches her back and rubs her breasts against my chest. I want to feel her skin rubbing against mine, but there are entirely too many clothes in my way. I kneel to rid myself of my t-shirt while Aspen scrambles to unhook her bra and shimmy out of her top.

As soon as we're both topless, I cover her body again and begin nipping and biting on her shoulders.

"What's wrong? You in a hurry? No stamina?"

I growl. "Don't poke the dragon."

Her hand slips between our bodies and she squeezes my hard length until my eyes cross and I see double.

"Is this the dragon to which you're referring?"

"You're playing with fire," I grumble.

"Well, dragons are fire-breathing creatures."

I love her sassy mouth, but I've had all I can handle. I slam my lips down on hers and thrust my tongue into her mouth. She threads her fingers through my hair before tugging on the strands the way she knows I enjoy. I moan down her mouth.

Our tongues duel as my hands explore her curves. With her bra out of the way, I'm free to massage her breasts and pluck at her nipples to my heart's content. She wraps her legs around my waist and rubs herself against my hardness.

This won't last long if she continues to grind against me. I rip my mouth from hers before crawling down her body. I pop the button on her jeans and draw the zipper down. I keep my gaze locked on Aspen's face to assess her reaction. I don't want her regretting anything we do here tonight. To my relief, she bites her lip before lifting her ass so I can rid her of her pants.

I draw the jeans and panties down her legs making sure my hands glide along her skin the entire time. Goosebumps explode in my wake. Once she's naked and laid out before me, I stare at her – unsure of where to begin.

She points at me. "Your turn."

I waggle my eyebrows. "You want a show?"

"You think you can give me a show?"

I glide my hand down my chest to my waist, and her eyes flare. "I think I'll manage."

I whirl around and sway my hips. She claps and giggles while chanting my name. "Lyric. Lyric. Lyric."

I lean forward a bit and wiggle my ass as I drag my jeans down my hips giving her a peek of my boxer covered ass.

Smack!

I glance at her over my shoulder. "Did you slap my ass?"

She shrugs. "You were going too slow."

Too slow? She wants to get to the good stuff? You won't hear me complaining.

"Shows over," I announce before kicking off my boots and shoving my jeans and boxers down my legs. As soon as I'm naked, I leap on the bed.

Aspen giggles as she widens her legs. I brace myself above her with my hips cradled between her thighs. I nudge at her opening and her eyes close as she sighs.

I pause to kiss her lips before diving another inch into her. I freeze and pull out. "Shit. Shit. Shit."

Her eyes fly open. "What's wrong?"

"I forgot a condom."

"I'm clean and I'm on the pill, much to my mother's chagrin."

"Your mother doesn't want you on the pill? Never mind. A discussion for another time." I blow out a breath. "I'm clean, too, but are you sure?"

"It's you, Lyric. Of course, I'm sure."

Her words make me feel as if I've won the lottery and the prize is her. I hook one of her legs over the crook of my elbow opening her up to me even more before thrusting inside her. Heaven. This is what heaven feels like.

I thought I'd exaggerated how it feels to have Aspen wrapped around me, but I didn't. She's warm and tight, and I never want to leave.

I plunge further until I'm fully seated and pause to give myself a second. Otherwise, I'm going to blow before Aspen comes, which is unacceptable.

She wiggles and her walls tighten around me. "What are you waiting for?"

With her walls spasming around me, there's no way I have a chance at going slow. I pull out before slamming back in. Aspen's fingernails dig into my shoulders and her back arches.

"Yes, Lyric. Just. Like. That."

I have no problem following her orders. I thrust in and out of her until I don't know where she ends and I begin. All too soon I feel the telltale tingling in my spine. Damn it. I'm not ready for this to end.

My hand sneaks between us until I reach her clit. I rub circles around it until she's gasping for breath and chanting my name.

"Yes, Lyric. Yes." She squeezes me as she comes, and I can't hold myself back anymore.

I lose my rhythm and my thrusts become erratic as I fall into bliss. I collapse but manage to roll to the side before I can squish her.

She cuddles into my side and throws her leg over mine. I sweep her hair off her sweaty forehead before kissing her there.

"I love you. I've never stopped loving you."

Her eyes close and she smiles before she falls into sleep. Great. I declare my love and she falls asleep. At least, she's in my arms. A place I plan for her to never escape from.

Chapter 29

A sneak – someone who uses sly, underhand tactics to flee because she's too chicken to deal with reality

I SIGH AS I snuggle into my pillow, but it feels hard and not soft like the featherdown should feel. Why is my— My eyes fly open as memories of last night flood into my wake mind. Lyric kissing me. Lyric making love to me. Lyric declaring his love to me.

Escape! Escape! Escape! I need to get out of here before I end up confessing my love to Lyric. Hold on. Do I love Lyric? Crap. I do. Of course, I do. Duh. I never stopped loving him. This wasn't supposed to happen. This is why I told myself to stay away from him. Fat lot of good it did me.

I raise my arm and head off of his body and he grunts. I freeze with my head and arm in the air until he settles again. Time to move. I roll out of the bed and hurry to the door. My boobs bounce, and I realize I'm naked. Shit. I need clothes.

Although no one in town will mind me running around naked, I have no desire to have pictures of me and my flabby ass plastered all over Facebook. And you can bet your bottom dollar, they'd be posted before I could make it home.

"Winter Falls doesn't have a chapel."

"She'll build one if it will ensure you get married and start pushing out grandchildren."

My stomach rolls and I feel sick. Grandchildren? I don't know if Lyric and I are permanent, let alone if we plan to have children. Except, a little voice in my head reminds me, you did let him make love to you without a condom last night. *Shut up! I don't want to hear it!*

"Uh oh, we better table the grandchildren discussion. Aspen looks like she's going to throw up all over the porch." Juniper wrinkles her nose and steps away from me.

"Come on, let's go to the treehouse. It has a heater and you're in your bare feet." Ellery links her arm with mine and drags me toward the backyard.

"Do you know why the treehouse has a heater?" I ask my sisters.

"Because Dad put one in," Lilac answers in her matter-of-fact voice.

"Because Mom told him to because she knew we were using the treehouse as a love shack," I inform them and watch with glee as their faces turn to disgust.

"Why would you tell us that?" Ellery asks.

"If I have to hear it from Mom, you're sharing in my misery."

"What are we talking about? The treehouse is a love shack?" Lilac asks as she looks around in confusion.

Ashlyn throws her arm around her shoulders and leads her to the treehouse. "Big sis, there is much you have missed in life."

We climb into the treehouse. Juniper carries Waffles up the steep stairs, while Ashlyn gets the heater going. We settle on the various pieces of furniture in the room, but I notice everyone leaves the mattress alone.

"I never understood why there was a mattress in here. Now, I'm concerned about the number of times I laid on it while studying." Lilac purses her lips while staring at the offending piece of material.

"There's no reason for concern. Mom always made sure there was a box of condoms in here." Juniper points to a drawer in one of the side tables.

"Were all of you having sexual liaisons in here?" Lilac asks.

Ashlyn raises her hand. "Not me."

Juniper bumps her shoulder. "Only because someone thought he'd be robbing from the cradle if you two went beyond friendship."

Ashlyn squares her shoulders. "Which is why I don't understand you, Aspen."

"Wait. What? I never touched Rowan, I promise."

Ashlyn rolls her eyes. "I know you didn't. You were too busy being obsessed with Lyric."

"I wouldn't say obsessed," I mumble, although she's not exactly wrong. There may be a whole bunch of school notebooks in my childhood bedroom with the name Aspen Alston scrawled in them and covered with hearts.

"Listen up," my little sister says in a commanding voice I've never heard her use before. "It's time to tell it like it is."

"Finally. I'll get my list." Lilac grabs her phone, but Ellery smacks her hand and shakes her head at her.

"I think we can all agree Aspen is being an idiot regarding Lyric. The question I have is why."

I roll my eyes. "Maybe because my life is in Dallas and Lyric's life is here. He's the Chief of Police. He'll never leave Winter Falls. I don't know how many times he told me he'll never leave."

Ellery raises her hand. "May I begin?" At Ashlyn's nod, she continues, "Why do you think your life is in Dallas?"

"I don't think my life is in Dallas, it is in Dallas."

"Except you can buy *Fall Into a Good Book* from Saffron and stay here."

Of course, she knows about Saffron's offer. At this point, everyone in town probably knows. The knowledge doesn't stop me from asking, "How do you know Saffron wants to sell me the bookstore?"

She ignores my question. "I remember when we were kids, and you spent all your spare time in Saffron's store. You always claimed you were going to own it when you got big."

I wrinkle my nose as I think back. "I did? I don't remember—" I cut myself off when a memory of me telling Saffron I'll buy her store when she gets too old pops into my mind. Those memories had all but disappeared.

"And the insurance settlement is way more than you need to purchase the store. You'd have a nice cushion for the leaner months," Lilac declares.

I scan the room. "You know about the insurance payment, too?"

"What can I say? Mom can't keep a secret to save her life," Ellery says.

"But don't worry. She didn't tell anyone else, and she swore us to secrecy," Juniper adds.

"Because you can keep a secret."

"Of course, I can keep a secret." Lilac is obviously offended by my question. "I have signed numerous non-disclosure agreements in my work."

"No one was talking to you, Robot Sister." I point to Ellery, Juniper, and Ashlyn. "I meant them."

"You'd be surprised what secrets I can keep." Juniper has my interest piqued now, but Ashlyn speaks before I have a chance to dive into Juniper's supposed secrets.

"I would move anywhere in the world to be with Rowan." She wipes at her eyes where tears are forming. "For the man I love, I'd move to the moon with a smile on my face. But you? You have the man you love practically begging you to be his and what do you do? You run away from him after he declares he's always loved you."

The tears spill over and down her cheeks. I rush to her and wrap her up tightly in my arms.

"I'm sorry, Ashlyn. Rowan's a fool if he doesn't want you. You deserve better."

She pushes me away. "I know I do. I'm officially giving up on him. From this moment on."

I squeeze her hand. "Good for you."

"Don't you get it? You don't have to give up on the man you love. You only have to move back home to a town you love." I open my mouth to deny it, but she wags her finger at me. "Nope, no lying. Plus, we're here. And we've missed you."

"I—"

This time it's Lilac who cuts me off. "Don't say anything now. You shouldn't make decisions after a night of passion."

Behind her, Ellery mouths *night of passion?*

"Consider all the options and various scenarios before you make a decision. Don't rush into anything. You have time."

I nod at Ellery's words. She's right. I shouldn't rush into a decision, but she's not right about time. I don't think I have much of it before Lyric starts pressuring me to return home. After all, he declared his love to me last night less than a month after we became friends again.

Chapter 30

Algebra – a method of torture for schoolchildren with no apparent everyday application

I CRINGE WHEN I open the front door to find Lyric standing there. I may have avoided him for the past day, which isn't easy in the small town of Winter Falls. Especially when any shop owners are quick to tattle on me when I 'happen' to rush into their store whenever I spot Lyric on the street. Stupid Project Weston.

Lyric's grin is tentative, and I hate myself a little. I'm such a bitch. Making this wonderful man I love insecure about himself because I'm messed up in my head about what to do is unfair to him.

"You must be here for Sunday dinner?" Mom, the matchmaker, strikes again.

"No, he isn't," the woman herself says as she comes up behind me.

She places a hand on my shoulder and shoves me. I wasn't expecting the move and end up flying out the door onto the porch.

I whirl around to glare at her. "What are you doing?"

"I'm making sure I have grandchildren in the near future."

I groan. "I never said I want children."

"Don't tell me you don't want mini versions of Lyric with sky blue eyes and brown wavy hair running around because I won't believe you," she huffs and slams the door in my face. In My. Face.

"I think I've been disowned."

Lyric lifts a picnic basket. "Don't worry. I've got something better than Sunday dinner."

I raise an eyebrow. "Impossible. Mom was making her famous fried chicken and coleslaw."

The door opens, and Mom shoves a container into my hands. "No more excuses."

I lift the container to my face and groan when I inhale the scent of the fried chicken. "I don't understand how my mom makes the best fried chicken in the world when she's not even from the South."

"Because she's your mom." Lyric takes the container from me and places it in the picnic basket. I try to peek at what else is in there, but he nudges me out of the way.

"Come on," he says and holds out a hand. "We're hiking to the falls for our picnic."

"Are you asking or telling?"

"I have food and, let's face it, your mom isn't letting you back in the house anytime soon."

I take his hand with a snort. "At least now I understand why Mom insisted I put on shoes for dinner. I thought she'd adopted another squirrel from Forest's store."

Lyric chuckles. "After what happened last time?"

"She claims she had no idea squirrels collect rattlesnake skins."

"I would have paid to have been a fly on the wall when your dad found the skin and thought it was a live snake."

I shiver. "It was horrible. Dad was whacking the hell out of the skin while Juniper screamed at him for being a murderer. Meanwhile, Lilac was jotting down notes about how 'normal' humans respond to threats and Ashlyn was crying hysterically in the corner."

He chuckles as we reach the entrance to the trail to the falls. "Your family is awesome."

"Do you miss your parents?"

Mr. and Mrs. Alston are on a year-long voyage to find themselves in Bali. I feel a bit guilty about it since I'm the one who recommended Mrs. Alston read *Eat, Pray, Love*. In my defense, I didn't think she'd use it as a guidebook.

"They'll be back before Christmas. In the meantime, they phone every week and send texts several times a day."

"Bali is supposed to be gorgeous. Do they send pictures?"

He shivers. "Don't ask. Just don't."

I laugh. I can guess what kind of pictures his parents send. They don't have a problem discussing their sex life with their children any more than my parents do. In fact, all of the town residents who are our parents' age or older are this way.

We climb the hill to the falls and make our way to a clearing from which we can observe the waterfall and the river. Lyric lays out a blanket, and I use the opportunity to peek into the basket.

"Someone went all out." In addition to the fried chicken and coleslaw, there are club sandwiches, a bucket of potato salad, fresh cherries, chocolate chip cookies, and a bottle of wine.

I remove the wine and some wine glasses. Real glasses since plastic is equal to blasphemy in Winter Falls.

Lyric doesn't talk as he prepares plates of food for us, which isn't normal for him. He may be a big, strong guy but he isn't the silent type.

"What's wrong?" I ask since I won't enjoy this wonderful spread of food he prepared if he's all grumpy and silent the whole time.

He chuckles, but he is not amused. "You seriously have to ask? I told you I love you and you snuck out of my house the next morning."

"Wow. You didn't ease into the topic at all."

"You asked. I'm not going to lie to you. I will never lie to you."

"I am sorry I snuck out on you."

"You are? Then, why have you avoided me for the past day?"

"Believe it or not, there's more going on in my life than our 'relationship'."

"Air quotes? Really? I don't know about you, but if I have sex with someone, we're in a relationship."

What is he getting at? "If you're asking if I had a bunch of one-night stands over the past ten years, I didn't."

He holds up his hand. "I do not want to ever hear about the men you've been with who weren't me." He pauses. "Unless you're currently in a relationship, then I want to know."

"Seriously?" I screech. "First, you accuse me of being a slut and now I'm a cheater."

He rubs a hand over his face. "This is coming out all wrong." He squeezes my hands. "I know you're not slut or a cheater, Sunshine."

My shoulders relax, and I slump forward. "Yeah, I know. There's a chance I'm being a tad bit bitchy to avoid the topic of conversation."

He leans forward and kisses my cheek. "It's okay. I know how stressed you must be after your talk with Saffron about buying the store."

And this is the point in the conversation when I have to tell him about the insurance money. I don't want to have this conversation in the first place, but I really don't want to have it when I'm unclear about what I'm going to do.

"There's more," I begin. When Lyric nods at me to continue, I explain, "My insurance company called. Their investigation is finished. They're going to send me a check for the amount they owe me."

He smiles. "That's awesome, Sunshine."

I rear back. "You think so?"

"Of course. Now, you have the cash to buy *Fall Into A Good Book*." I raise an eyebrow and he backpedals. "Or return to Dallas and rebuild your business, whatever you decide."

Silence falls until he admits, "I have to confess I'm relieved."

"Relieved? Were you worried I'm an arsonist?"

"Oh, I know you enjoy setting fires."

"I'm not some pyromaniac. The fire was an accident." I snarl. "I only meant to set off the fire alarm."

"You could have studied for the algebra test instead."

"Why? No one in the real world uses algebra in their daily life. Talk about a waste of time."

"You and your crusade against math."

I shake my finger at him. "Nuh uh. Math is fine. I use it all the time for my business, but algebra and trigonometry? What use are they? And what is trigonometry anyway? Don't ask me. I haven't the faintest clue."

"Maybe because you cheated off me in class and never learned what it was?"

I shrug. "Whatever."

"Shall I clarify what I meant about being relieved before you get up on your soapbox about mathematics curriculum in high school?"

"Since there aren't any soapboxes here in the woods, you may proceed." I flourish my hand like I'm the Queen granting him permission to speak.

"I thought you were upset because I told you I love you."

I roll my eyes. "Why would I be upset when the man I love tells me he loves me?"

When his smile stretches from ear to ear, I realize what I said. "I didn't mean—"

He slams his hand over my mouth. "Nope. You're not allowed to take it back." I lick his hand and he yanks it away.

"What I meant to say is, it doesn't change anything," I clarify.

"What do you mean?"

"My loving you doesn't factor into my decision on whether or not I'm going to buy the bookstore."

He cocks an eyebrow. "You haven't made up your mind yet?"

I glance away from him to stare into the water, so he doesn't witness the confusion on my face. I know I've been practically screaming from the rooftops about how I'm returning to Dallas the minute the insurance money arrives, but now the money's here, I'm unsure. My stupid sisters and their logical arguments.

I straighten my back as if readying for battle before I force myself to look at Lyric. He's staring at me with hope in his eyes, which does not make what I'm going to say any easier, but here goes.

"I don't know."

Chapter 31

Imploring – requesting someone to do what you want. Not to be confused with begging, which a Chief of Police would never do

LYRIC

My heart stops at her words. *I don't know.* She's not dead set on leaving this town in her rearview mirror. This is my chance to convince her to stay. Subtle can take a hike.

I cradle her face with my hands and say the one word I've wanted to say since I realized she didn't desert me a decade ago the way I thought she had, "Stay."

"What about my life in Dallas?"

I kiss her nose. "Do you want to live in Dallas? Do you miss your friends there?"

She cringes, and I go in for the kill.

"Do you not have good friends there?"

Now, she frowns. "Why does everyone keep asking me about my friends in Dallas? So, I don't have a gazillion friends there. It doesn't make me a loser."

"No one's saying you're a loser."

"It sure feels like it sometimes." She juts out her bottom lip in a pout.

I bite her lip before soothing the bite with my tongue. "I don't think you're a loser."

"Yeah." She giggles. "Because you want to get in my pants."

"Your pants, your skirt, your dress. I'm an equal opportunity bottoms remover."

I kiss the spot below her ear that makes her sigh before whispering into her ear, "Stay."

She shoves me away, and I end up flat on my back. "No using sex to get your way."

I waggle my eyebrows at her. "But I promise to make it fun."

She slaps my shoulder. "I know you would." I puff out my chest. "But I need to make this decision while not under the influence of your masculine wiles."

"My masculine wiles?"

"I'm being serious."

I sit up. "Okay, let's discuss this."

"You're going to be serious?"

I give her my cop face. "I can be serious."

She points to my face and makes a circle. "Are you trying to be serious or doing a smoldering look?"

"This is my cop face."

"No wonder ninety-five percent of the woman in this town voted for your election."

I tilt my nose in the air. "Because I am an excellent officer of the law."

"I can't believe the kid who won the golf cart race five years in a row is the Chief of Police."

"What's wrong with the golf cart race? It wasn't illegal. Okay, maybe souping up the batteries and tearing through the corn crop wasn't one-hundred percent legal, but we didn't harm anyone. Besides, it was six years in a row."

She barks out a laugh. "Thanks for proving my point, Mr. Speed Demon."

"No one's a speed demon in a golf cart." I wiggle my eyebrows at her. "Except for me."

She rolls her eyes. "Will you be serious for a moment?"

"Sunshine, I'm totally serious. I want you to stay. I'll beg you to stay at this point."

"What if this small town isn't enough for me?"

I knew this was coming. I can't count the number of times we fought about leaving town when we were in college. Aspen had her sights set on moving to the big city and making her mark there. While I was dead set on staying in town and becoming the Chief of Police. A feat I managed at the age of thirty. I'm thirty-three now, though, and I realize there are things in life more important than the badge I wear or the power I wield.

"Then, I'll come with you."

Her jaw falls open and she pretends to clean out her ear. "What did you say?"

"Don't act so surprised."

"How am I supposed to act? You claimed and I quote here." She lowers her voice and imitates mine, "'I won't leave Winter Falls until the place burns down, and even then, I'll stay to rebuild'."

I pinch her chin. "I was also twenty-three at the time. I'm sure you've learned some lessons in the past ten years."

"Yeah." She snorts. "Don't believe a man when he says he won't pressure you into staying."

I raise my hands in surrender. "Did I or did I not just tell you I'm willing to move to Dallas to be with you?"

She shrugs. "You did, but I don't know if I believe you."

"I'm serious." I'm also starting to sound like a broken record at this point.

She sighs. "How can I ever believe you? You wouldn't even consider leaving after college."

I admit I was a bit stubborn at the time, but things have changed.

"I've changed."

"Prove it."

Challenge accepted.

"My chief term expires in January, and I already told Mayor Forest I may not run for re-election. I've been grooming Peace for the chief of police position, and I think he'll do a good job. I've also found a nice, young couple who want to rent my house for a year."

Her mouth drops open and she stares at me. When I don't flinch, she whispers, "You're serious?"

"As serious as I am about making sure Lennon never sells absinthe in *Electric Vibes*."

"Like a dog with a bone," she mutters.

"And, let's face it," I add, "Waffles can't live without me anymore."

She mutters something about how dogs being loyal pets is all cat propaganda before asking me, "But what would you do in Dallas?"

"I have an application in with the Dallas police department."

Her eyes widen and she shouts, "What? When did you apply to the Dallas police force?"

"A few weeks ago, when I realized you didn't abandon me."

I haven't told a single soul in town about the application, since I didn't want to put pressure on my fragile relationship with Aspen. But since she still loves me, I'm thinking honesty is the best policy.

She frowns. "I should have stayed and talked to you instead of running away like some romance heroine done wrong."

I palm her neck and draw her near until our foreheads touch. "As much as I hate how we were apart for the past ten years, I think it was better for us as people and for our relationship."

Her nose wrinkles. "You do?"

"You were the only woman I'd ever been with. The only girlfriend I'd ever had. I'm not saying I would have wondered how it was to be with other women, but I am saying I don't need to wonder now. You are perfect for me, and I'm not letting you go."

"What if I don't want to live in Dallas? What if I want to travel the world in a van?"

"Then, Sunshine, I'll sell the house and buy you the best damn van money can buy."

"You'd leave everything to become a nomad with me?"

As much as I'd love to stay in Winter Falls and raise our family here, I love Aspen more. I know how it feels to miss part of my heart for a decade. I'm not going back to the empty life I lived without her.

I squeeze her neck. "You're not listening. I'd do anything for you. And, if you want to go on an adventure in a van, I'm in. On one condition."

"Which is?"

"I will not be filming everything we do to put on social media. I draw the line at making our lives a public spectacle."

She cocks her eyebrow. "Because our lives won't be a public spectacle if we live in Winter Falls."

"Sunshine, the people of Winter Falls aren't the public. They're our friends. Our family. The people who will always have our backs no matter what happens."

"They're also the people who are sneaking up behind you to try and eavesdrop on our conversation."

I already heard my brother and his big feet clomping through the bush. I was hoping to finish this conversation before he arrived.

"Go away, River!"

"Then, I can stay?" Phoenix asks, and I groan.

"You want to trade your sisters for my brothers?" I ask Aspen and she giggles.

"As long as Phoenix lets me play with his goats, I'm in," Juniper shouts.

"Those goats aren't pets," Phoenix grumbles.

"Here!" Ellery throws a swimsuit at Aspen. "Get changed."

"I should have known Mom wouldn't leave us alone all afternoon," Aspen mutters.

"Yee-haw!" Ashlyn hollers before jumping in the water with a big splash.

I might have been able to get rid of River and Phoenix, but there's no way I can convince the West sisters to leave. I may be the Chief of Police, but none of Aspen's sisters recognize my authority. They think of me as Aspen's boyfriend, Lyric, and nothing more.

I kiss Aspen and stand. "Time to show these people who the boss of these falls is." I snap my jeans open and Aspen screeches.

"No skinny dipping with my sisters around."

I wink at her as I drag my zipper down. She jumps to her feet and stands in front of me to block her sisters' view.

"Why, Sunshine, are you guarding my modesty?"

"You? Modest? No. I'm saving myself from a gazillion discussions about your anatomy."

I nip her earlobe. "Good thing I'm wearing swimming trunks then."

She whirls around and punches me in the stomach. "You could have told me."

"And ruin the fun? When have you ever known me to ruin the fun?"

"I guess I'll go get changed."

"Do you need me to protect you?"

She rolls her eyes. "Because I've never changed in these woods before?"

I wrap an arm around her and haul her near before she can escape. "Promise me you'll think about what I said."

"It's probably the only thing I'm going to think about until I make a decision. Bye-bye sleep."

I lean down to whisper in her ear, "I can always sneak into your bedroom and help you get to sleep."

She shoves me away. "Stop making me crazy."

I chuckle and kiss her hair. "Get changed. I promise I won't say another word about the future today. Let's have ourselves some good old-fashioned fun."

"At least with the Chief of Police on our side, we won't spend the night in jail," she says before running off.

"Don't count on it, math hater!" I shout after her.

Chapter 32

Good-bye – a parting of ways that isn't necessarily the end

I STARE DOWN AT the open suitcases on my bed. What am I doing? Is this what I want? To go back to Dallas and leave my family behind? To leave Lyric behind?

Lyric. Like the chicken I apparently am, I haven't told him my decision yet. My phone beeps, and I smile as I read the message.

Hey, girl! I heard you're on your way home. Can't wait to see you at the bar on Thursday night.

See? I'm not a total loser who has no friends.

My phone pings with another message. This one doesn't bring a smile to my face.

Ms. West,

As discussed during our telephone conversation, if we can't begin the repairs this week, then we won't be able to fit you into our schedule until April. Please confirm you will be on site on Wednesday.

Ah, yes. Now I remember why I'm rushing off to Dallas. If I don't begin with the repairs on my building now, I'll have to wait seven months. I'm not willing to live in limbo for seven months. *You can always sell the building,* a little voice in my head whispers.

I ignore the voice even if it is right. I only need to sell the building for the price of this year's property taxes and I'll break even. More than break even if I consider the big, fat check the insurance company deposited in my account last week.

"No!" I insist. I need to do this. I need to return home and figure things out despite the word home not feeling right in regard to Dallas anymore.

Continuing with my chicken tendencies, I send Lyric a message instead of calling him.

We need to talk.

About how you're leaving?

Drat! How did he find out? I swore my family to secrecy. There's only one other person who could possibly be the tattletale. Saffron. Naturally, the bookstore owner knows I'm leaving, too, since I can't exactly hit the road without letting the person I've been working for this past month know first.

Come to your window.

I rush to the window. Sure enough, Lyric is standing in my backyard staring up at me and he brought his grumpy, unhappy face.

"Why didn't you come around to the front door?" I shout down at him.

"Because you would let me in?"

"I deserved that. But, yes, I would have let you in."

He frowns before sauntering off to the front door. And, maintaining my whole chicken-shit routine, I keep my feet planted in my old bedroom until he knocks on the door.

"Come in!"

Lyric enters but stops two steps into the room when his gaze lands on the two suitcases open on the bed.

"You really are leaving. I was hoping this was some fantasy story concocted by the town in their whole Project Weston scheme."

The town? Note to self: Saffron's vows of silence are completely meaningless.

"I'm leaving." The admission causes my stomach to cramp.

"On Sunday, you told me you love me, and you didn't know what you were going to do. It's Tuesday, and you're all packed up and ready to go. Did you even consider staying?"

I fist his t-shirt in my hands. "It's the only thing I've thought about since you asked me to stay."

His hands cover mine. "Then, why are you leaving?"

I clear my throat and step away. I can't have this conversation while touching Lyric. We touch, and my mind forgets how to form words, let alone thoughts.

"I don't have a choice. The contractor has to start work on my building this week or it'll be spring before he has another opening."

His head drops and he rubs his neck. "Okay, I understand. What does this mean for us? Do you want me to follow you to Dallas? I can't leave until January."

I don't know. I don't want him to give up his life here. He's happy here. Who am I to rip him away from his friends and family? From the career he's always wanted? I don't want him to be miserable and resent me.

"Why don't we play it by ear?"

He grimaces. "Play it by ear?"

"I don't mean we're finished. I just mean I don't want you to give your life here in Winter Falls up yet."

He steps close and maneuvers me until I'm pressed against the wall. "The only thing I care about is you, Aspen." He cradles my face before kissing my nose. "Are you hearing what I'm saying?"

My heart pounds in my chest, and my hands tremble as I reach out to touch him. I grip his shoulders as I confess, "I love you, Lyric, but this is happening awful fast."

"We're a story twenty years in the making. Nothing fast about it."

"Let me re-phrase. Lyric and Aspen, the sequel, is moving fast."

He kisses the corner of my mouth. "Okay."

Emboldened by his agreement, I rush to reassure him. "It's not like we'll never see each other again. Thanksgiving will be here before we know it and then it's Christmas. And maybe you can visit me, too. Although, it won't be too comfortable sleeping in the middle of a construction zone."

A muscle in his jaw ticks. "You're staying in the building while it's being renovated. Is it safe?"

"The fire department cleared the building to begin renovations."

"Which could mean anything. Do you even have a door you can secure?"

I stare at the ceiling since I can't answer his question without lying.

"Fuck, Sunshine, if I can't be with you, you need to keep yourself safe. Promise me this." He pauses, and I force myself to look at him again.

"What?"

He leans his forehead against mine and closes his eyes. "Promise me you'll stay with a friend or get a hotel room if it's not safe."

"I promise."

"Are you two done saying good-bye? I need to get back to the inn," Ellery shouts through the door.

"I won't miss my sisters interrupting us," I say.

Lyric chuckles. "Liar." He touches his lips to mine in the briefest of kisses before placing his hands on my shoulders and whirling me around. "Get those suitcases shut, woman," he orders before slapping my ass.

I throw the rest of my things into the suitcases willy-nilly and Lyric carries them downstairs. My parents and sisters are waiting in the living room to say goodbye.

"You should eat before you go," Mom says.

My stomach rolls at the idea of food. "I need to get on the road," I say instead of admitting the thought of eating makes me feel nauseous.

Dad picks up a suitcase and carries it outside without saying a word. Lyric follows with the remaining suitcases.

"I can't believe you're leaving Lyric," Ashlyn says.

I hug her. "I'm not. We're not over. We'll figure things out."

I release her to find Ellery shaking her head at me. "You know long-distance relationships don't work."

I don't respond. Her experience isn't the same as mine. At least, I hope not. I pull her into my arms. "It's Lyric," is all I say.

"I don't know why you can't leave Waffles with me," Juniper says when it's her turn to say goodbye.

I look down at Waffles who's sitting at the door waiting for me to let him out. "I think you have enough animals to keep you busy."

"You got that right," Ashlyn mutters.

After I hug Juniper, I move to stand in front of Lilac. Saying goodbye is always awkward with her. She's uncomfortable with displays of affection. I pat her on the shoulder.

"Goodbye, Lilac. Keep in touch."

She nods. "I'll send you an email each Friday afternoon with details of my week."

Behind her, Ashlyn rolls her eyes, but I smile at Lilac. "Thank you." I appreciate those weekly emails. I've actually missed them while I've been in Winter Falls.

"What about the loot?" Ashlyn asks before I can force my feet to move to the door.

I shrug. "We're at a dead-end anyway."

"I'm not giving up. There must be clues in town somewhere," she declares.

Ellery laces her arm with mine and we walk outside where Mom, Dad, and Lyric are waiting by the car.

"I can't believe Old Man Mercury lent you his car," she whispers.

"I didn't even know he had a car."

"I think it's his way of ensuring Aspen returns to Winter Falls and solves the Mystery of the Black Hat Bandit's Missing Loot," Ashlyn declares.

"You're going to have to come up with a shorter name," I tell her.

"I'll work on it."

My sisters stay on the porch while I approach the car with Waffles. My dog darts straight to Lyric who scratches him behind the ears before opening the back door for him to scramble inside.

Dad hugs me. "Don't be a stranger, baby girl." He releases me and his gaze finds Lyric. "Although, something tells me you won't be." He winks and walks to the porch to join my sisters.

Mom wraps me up tight and sways from side to side. "I'll miss you, baby girl."

"At least now you'll have more time to concentrate on the love lives of your other daughters."

She frowns as she pulls away. "Their love lives are pathetic," she murmurs before joining Dad on the porch.

And now I'm alone with Lyric.

He opens his arms and I walk into them. I inhale his crisp, outdoor scent one last time.

"Call me when you arrive. And, if you get tired, make sure you pull over to rest."

"I'll be fine, Lyric. I promise."

"I love you," he murmurs before letting me go to open the car.

"I love you, too," I tell him once I'm settled behind the wheel.

I switch on the car and slowly back out of the driveway. I roll down the window and wave as I put the car into first gear and drive away.

I bite my tongue to hold in the tears until the town limits of Winter Falls are beyond me. Then, I let the tears fall uninhibited down my cheeks as I drive away from my home.

Chapter 33

Curve – a deviation from your intended path. Sometimes bad. Sometimes good. Sometimes fantastic.

I ROLL OVER AND cuddle my pillow to my chest. I breathe deeply and settle in for another hour of sleep. My nose wrinkles. My pillow doesn't smell like lavender as it should. And my blanket is scratchy. What the hell?

My eyes fly open, and I scan the room. This isn't my bedroom back in Winter Falls. It's a hotel room. Of course. How could I have forgotten? I left Winter Falls yesterday for Dallas. I'm staying in this cheap motel outside of the city before driving back to my building to assess the damage.

I had considered driving straight to my place, but it was dark outside, and I did promise Lyric I wouldn't stay if it was dangerous. How can I tell if it's dangerous if it's too dark to see? Thus, a hotel room for the night.

My phone beeps and I squint to read the text.

Good morning, Sunshine.

Sigh. I wish I was waking up in Lyric's arms instead of this – I sniff – cigarette-smelling hotel room. You made your bed, Aspen. Now, it's time to lie in it.

I message Lyric good morning before rolling out of bed to ready myself for the day.

Within fifteen minutes, I'm back on the road again with a free bagel and orange juice. Mercury will probably kill me when he finds out I've been eating and drinking in his pristine 1971 Dodge Charger. What is he doing with a muscle car anyway? This car would never pass the gasoline engine regulations in Winter Falls.

Since the traffic isn't too bad for a Wednesday morning, I find myself driving down my street forty-five minutes later.

"What do you think, Waffles? Is the building still standing?"

He yawns; completely uninterested in what I'm saying. He's probably dreaming of belly rubs from Lyric and treats from Juniper.

I'm not sure what condition the building will be in. It was still sealed off when I fled town. I couldn't sleep in my apartment while the fire was being investigated, and I had no money to my name. Thus, my hurried getaway to Winter Falls. Was it only a little over two months ago when I left?

I turn into the alleyway behind the businesses on the street and park behind my building. I exit the car with my gaze averted. *Stop being a chickenshit*, Aspen. I take a deep breath, straighten my back, and force myself to look up at the building.

I gasp at the vision before me. Holy guacamole. It is way worse than I thought it was. Somehow my memory has made the fire into less of a problem than it actually was.

I don't know much about construction, but this structure doesn't scream safe to me. Before I can investigate further, a truck pulls to a stop next to me. I smile at my contractor, Jimmy, as he slams his door.

"Ms. West."

"Aspen," I correct as we shake hands.

"You ready to do a walkthrough?" he asks without further ado.

I wish I could say no, but I can't. Time to get this show on the road. I motion to the building.

He takes an electric screwdriver from his truck and marches to the door. Except it's not a door. It's a piece of plywood across the space where my backdoor used to be. The situation just keeps getting better and better. He sets the wood to the side, and I follow him into the building.

I immediately start coughing as the smell of smoke hits me. I pull my t-shirt up over my mouth and nose as I study the room and its contents. The back storage room is a total loss. All the books have been burnt beyond recognition. I can't salvage anything here.

We move on to the front of the store. It's dark in here as the windows and door are covered with plywood since all the glass was destroyed during the fire. Jimmy switches on his flashlight and shines it around the area.

Great. It's not any better in here. Whatever wasn't destroyed by the fire was ruined by the water used to fight the fire. I hope my apartment is in better shape than this.

It isn't. Although the fire didn't reach this floor, the fireman must have doused the area with water to keep the fire from spreading as everything is waterlogged. And ruined. None of my furniture is salvageable. The only things I might be able to save are my dishes. Big whoop. I bought those at a garage sale ten years ago.

"I was planning on living in my apartment above the store during the renovations," I mumble to myself, but Jimmy hears me.

"Yeah." He scratches his neck. "That ain't gonna happen."

I sniff to stop the tears from falling. I put years of blood, sweat, and tears into building my business and making this apartment my home and it's gone. Every single bit.

"Can I say something?"

I nod at him to go ahead.

"Why don't you start new somewhere else? Renovating this place is going to take months. Months during which you won't have any income or a place to live."

"I can't. I can't carry the cost of the renovation and start somewhere new."

He clears his throat. "I'm willing to take this building off of your hands."

As soon as the words are out of his mouth, I realize this is what I want. I don't want to spend months renovating this business while I'm hundreds of miles away from Lyric. Why? This apartment where I crash after working twelve to fourteen-hour days at the bookstore isn't my home. It's a crash pad. Nothing more. Nothing less.

The one 'thing' making this place a home is Waffles, and he howled for most of the drive away from Winter Falls yesterday making his opinion on where he wants to live perfectly obvious. As if I didn't already know.

I study Jimmy for a moment. "Let's go get a coffee and talk numbers."

An hour later, I'm shaking his hand with a deal secured for him to purchase my building as well as the café I bought next door.

"I'll have my lawyer contact you," I tell him as we return to our vehicles.

He lifts his cap to me. "It's been a pleasure doing business with you, Ms. West."

I collapse into the driver's seat of the car. "Waffles, we're going home." He barks in response.

I switch on the motor. "Off we go!" He gives me his doggy smile.

The drive back to Winter Falls flies by compared to the drive down to Dallas two days ago. I stop twice to let Waffles out and have a bite to eat, but otherwise, I keep moving. I can't wait to get home.

It's nearly midnight when the sign for Winter Falls appears in my headlights. I slow down before pulling off to the side of the road. I haven't told anyone I'm on my way back. I'm sure Lyric would be happy to see me, but I don't know if I'm up to a 'big' talk right now.

There's only one thing to do. *The Inn on Main* it is.

Ellery lives in an apartment in the former carriage house, but it looks dark and closed up tight. I make my way to the entrance of the inn instead. When I don't find anyone at the reception desk, I go in search of her and find a light on in the kitchen.

"Knock! Knock!"

Ellery waves at me but keeps her gaze focused on her laptop. "I'll be out in two minutes to check you in."

"I didn't make a reservation. Are there any rooms available?"

Her hands freeze above the keyboard before she slowly lifts her head and a smile spreads across her face from ear to ear. "Aspen!"

She springs to her feet before tackling me to the ground. "You came back!"

"Shush! You're going to wake the entire town."

Her smile switches to a smirk. "You didn't tell anyone you were coming, did you?"

I shrug. "I feel like a fool. I drove all the way to Dallas just to have confirmed what everyone has been saying for weeks – Winter Falls is my home, not Dallas."

"You're not a fool." She stands before helping me to my feet. "But you do need to make a grand gesture to Lyric."

"A grand gesture? What kind of grand gesture?"

"I have some ideas. Let's ca—"

She doesn't manage to finish her sentence before Juniper and Ashlyn rush into the room.

"How did you know I was here?" I ask once we've hugged.

Ashlyn points to Juniper. "Someone was out walking one of her gazillion pets when she saw a Dodge Charger drive by."

"You didn't tell anyone else, did you?"

Lilac strolls into the room. "Just me."

"Don't tell anyone else," Ellery insists. "We're doing a grand gesture for Lyric."

I raise an eyebrow. "We?"

She waves away my comment. "You know what I meant. Aspen will hide away in the attic room here until it's grand gesture time."

Grand gesture time? I'm starting to get worried.

Ashlyn jumps up and down while clapping. "Awesome! I have some ideas."

I'm no longer getting worried. I am worried. I need to put the brakes on this.

"I bet if I sneak through Lyric's window naked, he will be happy." And, frankly, so would I.

"Nope. Not good enough." Ashlyn pulls out a notebook. "Let's begin."

I've passed worried and moved on to straight up fear. Ashlyn, the troublemaker, has a notebook. The entire town is in danger now.

Chapter 34

Grand gesture – a hell of a surprise. The good kind.

LYRIC

I sigh as I exit the police station. Main Street is crowded with residents and tourists alike waiting on the Mabon Festival Parade to begin. It's the reason I'm in Winter Falls today and not on my way to Dallas.

I know Aspen only left town a few days ago, but I already miss her. I rub my chest where an ache blossoms every time I think of her. Aspen may believe our relationship is new, but I disagree. I'm ready to dive into us being together. Forever, if I have my way. And I usually do.

"Chief," Forest rushes up to me.

I tilt my hat to him. "Mayor."

"We've got a situation."

Of course, we do. "What is it this time? Naked revelers? Or is Juniper protesting the use of horses again?"

Since we don't have many cars in town, horses are used to draw the carriages in the parade. Every time I turn around, Aspen's sister is complaining about something to do with how we're treating the horses. As if anyone in this town would ever mistreat an animal.

At Forest's head shake, I guess again. "Did Cayenne tie herself to the tree in the middle of the town square again?"

"I'm being serious," the mayor insists.

"Cayenne tying herself to a tree is serious. Do you not remember how long it took us to untie her?"

The entire town came out to give their advice on how best to not harm the tree. Add Cayenne deciding she needed to use the facilities, *right now!* and you have a disaster on your hands. At one point, Lennon offered her a pair of adult diapers. I don't want to even think about how he thought he'd get those on her.

Forest motions toward the grandstand across the square. Grandstand is a fancy word for a few rows of bleachers the town borrowed from the high school.

When I spot Mrs. West waving at me frantically, I break into a run. Those old bleachers aren't the most stable. I hope to hell they didn't collapse and trap someone. My eyes scan the crowd for any paramedics on duty.

I spot River. My brother's a part-time firefighter and has paramedic training. "River!" I shout across the crowd. He nods and falls in step behind me.

"What's going on?"

"I don't know. The bleachers may have collapsed."

His eyes widen and he grabs his walkie-talkie off his belt.

"The bleachers didn't collapse!" Forest yells at us.

"Then, what's the emergency?"

We arrive at the grandstand, and Forest points to a chair next to his on the raised platform.

"What's going on?"

Mrs. West is done waiting for me. She shackles my wrist and drags me to the platform. "You! Sit there!"

"I need to be on patrol," I tell her. I'm the Chief of Police. I can't sit on my ass while the entire police force is out doing crowd control.

"Sit down or I'll tell the entire world about the time I walked in on you—"

I have no idea to what she's referring. There are way too many times she busted me doing things I'd rather the entire town not know about.

"All right. All right."

I sit down and Forest takes the seat next to me. River sits behind me while Mrs. West returns to her place next to her husband.

"Where are the girls?" I ask her.

She winks. "You'll see."

I groan. I can imagine the type of float the West sisters would come up with. The first time they had a float in the parade they burned their bras. Fortunately, they weren't actually the bras they were wearing. Unfortunately, Ashlyn got a bit carried away and decided to throw her bra – while burning – into the crowd.

One of the first things I did as Chief of Police was outlaw any type of incendiary devices in town during a festival. Poor

Lennon still has a bald spot from where the bra hit him on the head.

I check my watch. It's noon on the dot. The parade should be starting. The bleachers are smackdab in the middle of town on the town square in front of the library and across from the courthouse and police station. It won't be long before the first participants reach us.

I tap my foot as I continue to scan the crowd for any problems. It appears as if every resident of Winter Falls is on the streets today, which isn't unusual. Except for... is that – I squint my eyes – it sure is. Mercury is here. Since when does the hermit attend town events?

The first participant of the parade is always the Mabon King and Queen. The couple wave and hand out candy apples from the back of their decked out golf cart. Next up is the high school marching band. I don't pay much attention. I'm too busy ensuring the crowd doesn't get out of control.

I smile when I hear the trombones to signal the intro of Christina Aguilera's *Ain't No Other Man*. Aspen loved this song when we were seniors in high school. She used to sing it to me all the time. Aspen. I rub my chest as the ache builds. Man, I miss her.

Someone starts singing, and I shake my head. I must be missing Aspen worse than I thought since the singer sounds exactly like her. I look up at the float to figure out who it is.

Wait a minute! It is Aspen singing. And dancing. With her sisters as backup singers. And holy smokes! What is she wearing? She resembles one of those women in that *Burlesque* movie she made me watch when we were in college.

Don't get me wrong. She's sexy as hell but maybe a little too sexy. I notice every man in the vicinity has his eyes glued to her chest. Except for Rowan. His eyes are zeroed in on Ashlyn who's shaking her ass as she dances.

I hope I'm nowhere near when that situation explodes. It appears detonation is imminent considering how red Rowan's face is. I can tell his teeth are clenched from across the street. But Rowan and Ashlyn are a problem for another day.

The question of today is: what is Aspen doing here? No. Wait. That's not the question. The question is: why is she not in my arms? I stand, intent on getting to her as quick as possible, but River holds me back.

"Let them finish. They worked their asses on this."

"What? How do you know?"

He shrugs.

"Did the whole town know about this?"

"You think the West Sisters could manage this on their own?" River asks.

"Yes." I have no doubt those five women can do anything they put their minds to.

"But they didn't."

"You've all watched me mope around town for the past week while knowing Aspen's in town."

He shrugs. "Apparently, she wanted to do a 'grand gesture'. Whatever the hell that means."

And now I understand why everyone insisted I sit on the grandstands instead of doing rounds. This town.

I shake off River's hold to go stand in front of Aspen's float where a crowd has gathered. Some are dancing while others sway from side to side with their phones raised displaying virtual lighters.

My fellow police officer, Peace, joins me. He slaps me on the shoulder.

"Your girl."

I know. She's crazy, but I love her.

Aspen's gaze locks on mine and she begins singing directly to me. She winks at me, and I can't help but laugh at her antics. I will never be bored with this woman in my life.

The song winds down, and the crowd cheers as if they were at a rock concert. Someone even throws a pair of underwear onto the float. I search the crowd to find the culprit and Lennon waves at me with a waggle of his eyebrows.

I don't know where the boxers came from, but thankfully, he's still wearing jeans on his bottom half. Public nudity may not be a crime in Winter Falls on most days, but during parades and festivals, we try to keep things PG-rated for the tourists.

Although guessing by how many of the female tourists are currently approaching Lennon, they wouldn't mind a bit of public nudity. He motions for the women to follow him and off he goes. I can only guess what they'll get up to. Better not to know for sure.

"Welcome home, Aspen!" her sisters shout, and my attention reverts back to the float where Aspen is staring at me while biting her lip.

Home? She's back for good? I raise an eyebrow at her, and she nods.

I hand my weapon to Peace. "Put this in the safe, will you? I'm officially off duty."

He chuckles. "You got it, Chief."

I don't wait for him to finish speaking before I run and take a leap to jump on the float.

The crowd chants, "Kiss her! Kiss her!"

Who am I to deny the crowd what they want? I cradle Aspen's face in my hands and meld my lips to hers.

Chapter 35

Surprise – impossible to do in a small town

LYRIC

"Ahem!" I ignore whoever's clearing their throat. I've got better things to do right now. "Ahem! Chief!"

Shit. I forgot I was the Chief of Police there for a minute. I tear my mouth away from Aspen's. Her lips are swollen from my kisses, and I'm tempted to dive right back in. Onlookers be damned.

"Chief!" River shouts again.

"What?" I bark.

He smirks. "I thought maybe you had a little surprise of your own for our Aspen."

I snarl at him. What a little shit. He knows I've been keeping the engagement ring I bought for Aspen in my pocket since the day she left.

"Unless you're going to chicken out."

"Yeah, Chief, you gonna chicken out?" Phoenix adds his taunt.

"My brothers are assholes," I tell Aspen.

"At least your parents aren't in town," she says and nods to her parents who are standing behind my brothers with expectant looks on their faces.

"Come on, Chief. Let's get this over with. The parade needs to keep moving," Forest yells.

I motion to Juniper who has control of the horses pulling the float. She crosses her arms over her chest, obviously refusing to signal the horses to giddy-up.

I grasp Aspen's hand. "Let's get out of here."

Her eyes sparkle. "I approve of this idea, Chief."

I move to the edge of the float, but before I can jump down, the crowd around the float moves until we're surrounded by a sea of townspeople.

"You're not going anywhere, son," a familiar voice announces.

"Dad?" I scan the crowd until my eyes fall upon my parents. "What are you guys doing here?"

"We wouldn't miss this for the world," Mom says.

Aspen groans. "Did everyone in the world witness me singing and dancing while wearing this bustier?"

"Not yet, but they will soon." Phoenix holds up his phone. "I recorded the entire act."

Her cheeks flame and I lean close to whisper, "The bustier is sexy as all get out. I have plans for it later."

Her eyes flare, and her cheeks darken further. She cocks her head and bites her lip. "Oh yeah? What kind of plans?"

I lower my voice and growl into her ear, "The kind requiring a bedroom without an audience."

Ellery clears her throat. "As much as I'm enjoying this, we really do need to get moving. The entire parade is stalled."

"Then, let's move," I tell her.

She snorts. "Juniper isn't moving this float until you …" she flourishes a hand, "you know."

That's the last time I buy jewelry in this town. I thought I was supporting the local economy not fueling the flames of gossip in town. I should have known better than to think Rain of *Bohemian Treasures* would keep her mouth shut. I search the crowd for our local jeweler. When our eyes meet, she shrugs as if she has nothing to do with my current predicament. Liar.

I throw out my arms. "You're serious. You're going to make me do this here and now?"

Aspen tugs on my sleeve. "Tell me you love me, I'll tell you I love you, and then they'll leave."

"Like the entire town doesn't know you two have been in love since you were sixteen," my mom shouts.

Aspen waves to her. "Hi, Mrs. Alston."

I study the crowd. Everyone is staring at me with expectant gazes, but they're not being nosy onlookers. No, the people of this town are genuinely happy Aspen and I have made our way back to each other.

Damn. I'm going to do this in front of everyone, aren't I?

I lower to one knee and grasp Aspen's hands.

"What are you doing?" she whispers.

"What's that? We can't hear you?" her dad, Daniel, yells.

"She asked him what he's doing," Ellery shouts back.

"Isn't it obvious? He's proposing in front of the entire town," Lilac says.

Juniper squeals. "Yeah! It's like a movie."

"Sorry," Aspen says. "I've tried to get rid of them but to no avail. I'm stuck with them now."

"Ah, big sis, we love you, too." Ashlyn sends Aspen air kisses.

I shake Aspen's hand to get her attention. "Can we get back to the matter at hand?"

"And what matter would that be?" she sasses.

"Aspen Cloud West, my sunshine, will you marry me?"

"You're not going to say anything corny like 'will you make me the happiest man on earth by saying yes'?"

I shrug, and she frowns. "This is disappointing. I was expecting more from you."

There's my sassy girl. I squeeze her hands.

"Aspen Cloud West, I have loved you since the day you shoved Love Hill into a mud pile when we were ten because she called me a booger. My love for you only grew in high school when you staged a war on mathematics classes with false fire alarms and fake injuries complete with blood, which I discovered was actually chocolate syrup. I loved you through college and your sit-ins and protests and petitions about the use of plastic in the cafeteria. And my love for you survived through ten years of separation during which both of us grew to become the people we are now."

She frowns. "Are you going to tell the entire world all of my secrets?"

"None of those things were secret," her mom yells.

"Have you heard enough, Aspen? Or do you want me to say more before I ask for your hand in marriage? Because I'll kneel here all day while the entire town stares at us until you say yes."

And I will. I wanted to propose with just the two of us at the falls where we first made love, but I've reconciled myself to the situation. I knew when I decided to stay in Winter Falls after college, privacy was not a virtue this town respects.

"What if I need to return to Dallas?"

"Then, I'll accept the job the Dallas police department offered me."

She whoops, "You got the job!"

"I got the job."

"What job?" River yells.

"Are you abandoning us?" Phoenix asks.

I glare at my brothers. "If I have to choose between you two and Aspen, Aspen's going to win every damn time."

And they know this. They're just trying to drive me crazy. Trying? They are driving me crazy.

Aspen squeezes my hands to gain my attention. "But I sold my building."

"You sold your building?"

She shrugs. "Yeah, it was a mess. Everything was destroyed. What wasn't destroyed by the fire was ruined with water damage."

"I'm sorry, Sunshine. I know how hard you worked to establish your business."

She smiles. "It's okay. I have somewhere I'd much rather be."

"Winter Falls? Or are we going on an adventure traveling around the world in a camper?"

Her nose wrinkles. "It'll be awful hard to travel the world in a camper when I have a bookstore to run here in town."

"You bought *Fall Into A Good Book?*"

I hold my breath as I wait for her answer. If she bought the bookstore, she's definitely staying. I didn't lie. I would travel the world with her, but I'd prefer to stay right here where we both belong.

"Signed the letter of intent yesterday."

"Who doesn't know Aspen was in town this week?" I roar my question at the crowd, and suddenly everyone finds the pavement fascinating.

"Blame me," Aspen says. "I swore them all to secrecy."

"Swearing the people of this town to secrecy usually doesn't mean a damn thing."

She winks. "Maybe not when you do it."

"What do you say, Aspen? Are you going to marry me?"

She rolls her eyes. "Of course, I'm going to marry you. I've been in love with you since you sat down next to me in first grade and offered me your chocolate pudding."

I jump to my feet and pick her up before twirling her around.

"Woo-hoo!" her mom shouts. "A son-in-law and a wad of cash on the same day? It must be my lucky day."

Aspen rolls her eyes. "I guess we know who won the Project Weston bet. Now, where's my ring?"

I set her down and grab the ring out of my pocket. She holds out her left hand, and I slide the ring onto her finger.

"I love you, Mrs. Soon-to-be Alston."

"I think you mean West-Alston."

"Whatever," I grumble. Like I care what her last name is as long as she's wearing my ring and sleeping in my bed.

"I love you, too, Lyric Journey," she whispers.

My lips find hers, and we seal our engagement with a kiss. I cut the kiss short when the crowd cheers.

"Do you think we can escape before the entire town springs on the float to congratulate us?"

She lifts her chin to Juniper. "We already have our escape route planned."

"Of course, you do."

Like I said, life will never be boring with Aspen by my side.

Chapter 36

To pine – to long for someone you can't have

ASHLYN

I sigh as I watch my sister and her brand-spanking-new fiancé sneak away. We stopped the float near the alley leading to the bookstore, and they jumped off and rushed away before the townspeople could follow them.

"Ten bucks says we don't see them again today," Ellery says.

Juniper snorts. "We'll be lucky if they come up for air for Sunday's family dinner."

"What a ridiculous bet. No one can have sex constantly for twenty-four hours," Lilac, aka Ms. Logic, points out.

I don't join in the bet. I'm too busy trying to tame the ugly green monster, aka jealousy. I shouldn't be jealous of Aspen. She's my big sister. She deserves love. She was broken-hearted for a decade because she thought the love of her life cheated on her. And Lyric wasn't much better, thinking Aspen had abandoned her.

I'm happy they ironed out their issues. I am. Truly, I am. But maybe I'm a teensy-weensy bit jealous the man I've been pining for since I realized what boys are good for barely acknowledges my existence.

Speaking of the man I'm pining for, I notice Rowan marching down the street. Judging by the lowered brows and clenched jaw, he's pissed. I'm surprised when he points his finger at me.

"You! Get your ass off that float this instant!"

I glance over my shoulder to see who he's talking to. Surely, it's not me. The man hardly deigns to speak to me. I know he knows I exist. We live in a small town where everyone knows everyone. Plus, he's friends with Aspen. He simply doesn't bother to interact with me.

My heart burns, and I rub a hand over my chest at the familiar ache.

"Ashlyn!" Rowan cries, and I whip my head up to find him standing next to the float glaring up at me.

"What? What is your problem? What did I do wrong now?"

"You seriously have to ask?"

Yes, I do. I may have annoyed the hell out of him by following him around like a puppy when I was a teenager, but I've grown out of that stage. There's not a thing he should be annoyed about with me now. Except for how I may sort of frequent his bakery more often than is good for my ass. But I pay for those treats, and it's money going into his pocket. He can't be annoyed with me for helping his business thrive.

I puff out a breath of air. "What are you talking about?"

His hand motions to my outfit. It's a killer outfit by the way. I'm wearing lace-up boots that go past my knees, a short leather skirt, and a bustier on top. The skirt is tight since I have a more than generous ass, but the bustier is loose because I apparently forgot to get in line when they were handing out boobs.

"Your outfit is inappropriate."

I snort. "Are you serious?"

He crosses his arms over his chest and my mouth waters at the vision of his bunched up forearms and muscular chest. The man may spend his days making mouth-watering treats, but he looks like he should be on the cover of some men's fitness magazine because he is f-i-n-e fine.

"Your ass is falling out of your skirt."

I pluck at the hem of my skirt. "I know I'm not skinny like other women, but it's rude to point it out."

"Your ass is fine."

I grimace. He doesn't mean fine the way I do. No, he's using fine as in 'it's okay considering you eat baked goods every single day and wouldn't know what a treadmill was if it hit you in the face'.

"What's not fine is your ass hanging out."

"Who the hell do you think you are? You're not my brother."

"Since you don't have a brother, I'm stepping in."

I cringe. Brother. He sees me as his little sister? All the days and months and years I've spent trying to show him how I've grown up to be a woman hasn't changed a thing. He'll always see me as a little sister. An annoying little sister he has to watch out for.

"Don't worry. I'm going home to change after this," I tell him, so he'll leave. I need him to leave before I break down in tears.

"Where are you going?"

"None of your business," I growl.

He cocks a brow and merely waits for my reply.

I throw my hands in the air. "If you must know, I'm going to Phoenix's farm to mind the animals."

While Phoenix is off celebrating, I'll be feeding his animals and mucking stalls. I sound like I feel sorry for myself, but I don't. Okay, maybe a little. I have to do all kinds of odd jobs in town in order to have enough money to pay my bills each month. It's not permanent, though. As soon as my business is up and running, I can stop cobbling together money from every job that comes my way.

And now there's one less daily expense to worry about. No more pastries from *Bake Me Happy* for me. Because I'm done with Rowan.

The pining for a man who sees me as his little sister stops now. I'm twenty-three years old. If he still can't see I'm a woman, there's no hope for us.

"Good," he nods and marches off without another word spoken.

No more, Ashlyn. *No more*. You're worth more than this.

I am done pining for the asshat formerly known as Rowan.

About the Author

D.E. Haggerty is an American who has spent the majority of her adult life abroad. She has lived in Istanbul, various places throughout Germany, and currently finds herself in The Hague. She has been a military policewoman, a lawyer, a B&B owner/operator and now a writer.

Printed in Dunstable, United Kingdom